Justine,

Beautifully

(The Infinite L

By: Kira Adams

The Infinite Love Series
Learning to Live
My Forever
Beautifully Broken
Against All Odds

Cover design by Cover Me Designs
Editing by Joanne LaRe Thompson

Don't forget—if you're not doing something you love, you're not really living!

Kira Adams

1

This is for all the people out there that aren't "normal". For all the broken souls out there who deserve love just as much as anyone. I dedicate this book to you.

Kira Adams

One – Memory Eraser

Jacqueline

My head fell back hitting the bathroom wall with a thud. I loved the feeling that came over me as an after effect. It was my own personal high. I exhaled loudly, my eyes still closed; reveling in the light headed feeling.

Even though I was emancipated at fifteen, and had been living on my own ever since, my routine had never wavered. Although it was the one thing I looked forward to most days, it was also something I was ashamed of.

I knew if I ever wanted to give myself fully to someone, they should be entitled to know. That's why I kept everyone at an arm's length away.

Parker Grant was the only other human being on this earth I had trusted enough to contemplate telling…but after he chose Madalynne, I saw no reason.

My entire life I had never felt worthy of love, yet found myself seeking it out due to my father's absence in my life, and my drug addicted mother.

When I was seven years old, my teacher Mrs. Edelson called Child Protective Services on my mother. My mother had forgotten to pick me up after school. I'm not talking late, I'm talking full on no call, no show. Who forgets to pick up their own child?

My father dipped out not too long after that; it all becoming too much for him. I heard from one of my mother's rants that he ended up somewhere in Mexico.

I was claimed by CPS and put into foster care at the age of thirteen after I called 911 because I found my mother passed out on the ground, crack pipe next to her, throw up all over the ground.

I spent two agonizing years in foster care before filing for emancipation. I had applied and been approved pretty quickly thanks to the amazing Godsend I had of a case worker, Trinity.

Luckily, I was an only child, so no other children had to be subjected to the hell I went through growing up.

The only person who even made my life worth living was my friend Travis. He was my pillar of support during my childhood years.

I met him in middle school and we spent almost every day together after that. He knew everything I had been through with my parents; he knew how difficult my life had been from day one.

He was the person I called the day I tried to kill myself. He was the person who saved my life. He stuck by me through thick and thin; the real definition of a friend.

At fifteen when I was granted emancipation, Travis convinced his parents to take me in, and knowing how close we were, they did. I thanked God every day for them. In return for my free pass I helped out by working in their stables.

What most would consider hard labor, I considered my fresh start and actually came to love the horses I cared for and the work that I did. It felt very fulfilling and helped center me.

Travis and his parents were also the only ones aware of my disorder. They handled me with kid gloves, making sure not to test me. They knew how quickly I could be triggered and shoot from zero to one hundred, and yet, they

5

still forgave me and reassured me that it's not my fault—just a result of my shitty upbringing.

While Travis likes to think he knows everything about me—he knows nothing of my biggest secret and I don't know that I want him to.

Travis has been there for me when no one else has. And even though I know he'd still accept me; the truth is far too hard to face.

"Well, are you going to get that or not?" She looks at me, a tired expression running the course of her face.

I nod slightly, slowly making my way to the front door, knowing with each step I take, danger closes in. I glance back at my mother one more time. Her eyes look sunken in, her blond hair hasn't been washed in over a week, and I wonder if she is aware of the stench perforating off her.

"Get to it!" She screams once she notices my hesitation.

The banging picks up volume, more urgent this time, and I know it's not good for me. After fumbling with the lock nervously and opening the door, he pushes it open roughly, knocking me out of the way. "What took so long?" He growls at my mother.

"I'm sorry baby!" She jumps up from the couch and embraces him; slapping me across the back of the head. "Jacqueline took her sweet time; it won't happen again." She turns her attention to me. "Go on to your room now."

I may be young, but I'm not naïve. I know exactly what is going to happen when I leave the room. They are going to get high as a kite together; my mother's drug of choice this week is meth. And then they will add weed into the mix a little later. That is what I don't want to think about—the possibilities of later. So I hurriedly race to my room, locking the door behind me. It's not like I can't still picture his sleazy grin and missing teeth or his dirty clothes and terrible stench. It was what I had nightmares about.

I had a close call a month ago when one of her "friends" came knocking at my door in the middle of the night. I lied there, perfectly still, frozen in fear as the handle jiggled and jiggled until eventually, it just stopped. It was the first night I locked my door and I've been doing it ever since.

Roger, the scumbag over now has crossed the line more than a few times with his vulgar language towards me. And one time he even walked in on me in the shower. He swore it was an accident to my mother; but I saw his eyes taking in my pre-teen body—and I was scared shitless.

The incident had occurred a few weeks ago and I am terrified to even be around him now. I press my ear to the door, relieved when I can still audibly hear my mother's voice.

I change into pajamas and climb into bed. I'm not asleep for more than 45 minutes when I hear the rattling of my door handle. My heart rate spikes in anticipation.

"Roger? Where are you?" I hear my mother's voice faintly. My fear accelerates knowing she isn't the one outside my door. The handle wiggles a few more times before I hear her again, only this time more clearly, "What the fuck are you doing?"

"Who are you talking to in that tone, woman?" Roger's voice rings through. Then I hear what sounds like his fist hitting her. I think my heart is going to jump out of my chest. I barely hear her now, but it is apparent that she is whimpering.

"I'm sorry baby. Just come back to the living room, we can order a pizza and watch a movie." I can see their shadows beneath my door frame.

"No one tells me what to do," I hear him exclaim before the sound of a second altercation grabs my attention.

"If you touch her, I'll kill you." My mother's concerned tone takes me by surprise.

The sounds of breaking glass and dishes startle me. I jump up from my bed, bracing myself against the wall. I want to be strong and check on my mom, but the sound of heavy footsteps is too terrifying. I can't move a muscle.

The jiggling of the door handle begins again, only this time it is more forceful; more anxious.

I crawl underneath my bed; for some reason it seems like the only space small enough he may not be able to reach me. I press myself against the wall, as close as I can get, right underneath the headboard.

I can hear what sounds like kicking at my door, taking my breath away. I close my eyes and cover my ears; it makes it feel less real that way.

Lee

I never intended to fall. In fact, when I boarded that plane back home, it was the furthest thing from my mind. It hit me like a ton of bricks the other night. We were just hanging out at our usual beach spot when she looked up at me and the moon glistened off her face just so, illuminating her undeniable beauty. I knew quickly on I would never meet anyone like Madalynne Johnson. Beauty, brains, and genuine? Yes, please. I could tell she was into me; it wasn't rocket science, but I knew what I wanted out of life; adventure and excitement. Without much effort I found that Maddy encompassed all of that and more.

I remember the first night I woke up in a cold sweat. I glanced over at Maddy, peacefully asleep beside me and it slowed my heart rate; calmed me down. The effect she had on me was unlike any I had ever felt before. It was a feeling of comfort and safety; it felt right.

Deep down I know she has a guy back home, but I try to avoid these thoughts. Eventually, a decision will be forced upon her, stay in Hawaii with me or leave for him. I've been making the most of our time together for this exact reason.

I glance down at her, making a mental note that she is still fast asleep. I gently sweep her long brown hair out of her face and kiss her on the forehead. She stirs a little from this before rolling over and dominating my side of the bed. I can't help but smile. Normally I would be in bed with her, snuggling, but I want to surprise her. I want to show her how much of an impact she has made on my life. I have never dated anyone I've felt this strongly about; meaning I never bothered to go the extra mile. Sleeping beauty over there is beyond worth it to me.

Earlier, I woke up at dusk and raced out to the closest pharmacy where I picked up a small box of chocolates and a card. I didn't even know what had gotten into me, but she had me smitten.

Little encouraging affectionate notes are scattered all over the ground; so unlike me. I never have to worry about the chase—girls fall all over me every day. Maddy fell as easily if not as quickly, but it wasn't the same on my end. I fought the attraction, the chemistry, and the passion, but knowing what I know—the other guy in her life is going to be getting out of Basic soon; has lit a fire up under my ass.

I grab the breakfast tray which is loaded with toast, bacon, eggs, and orange juice and make my way

11

back to my bedroom.

I sit down on the edge of the bed. I'm just about to wake her when I see her begin to stir. "What smells so good?" She asks through closed eyes.

"Open your eyes," I whisper, awaiting her response.

She rubs her eyes a few times before switching them to me. "Breakfast? You made me breakfast in bed?" She sits up excitedly, a surprised reaction taking over her face.

I nod without replying.

"What's the occasion?" She asks.

"Just 'cause," I reply simply.

She smiles a big grin before hastily grabbing the breakfast tray and immediately pigging out.

"I take it you were hungry?" I laugh, stretching. "Now I need a nap! I've been slaving away on your breakfast all morning and I didn't even get a thank you."

She rolls her eyes at me. "Shut up and kiss me."

I obey; closing the distance between us, I lower my lips to hers.

This is the woman I love. One of the only women I have ever loved. I am determined to make her mine, only mine.

"Brring," the shrill alarm screeched for what must have been the fourth time. I sighed dramatically before finally rolling over and silencing the obnoxious sound for good.

It had been two weeks since Madalynne made her decision; Parker; and exited my life forever. Heartbreak was not something I was familiar with. I let women close, but not close enough to ever hurt me...Maddy was the first.

No one prepares you for the pain associated with losing a loved one. Someone I had fallen into a routine with. Someone I let down my walls for. I could never regret a single moment spent with her though, because she showed me what real love was; she made me a believer.

My entire life I avoided love and any possibility of it, knowing just how messy it could be. Sex was enough for me and the affection I received from it held me over. She changed it all for me. The night on the beach with the bimbo, I knew—Maddy was going to change my life—I only hoped it was for the better.

I've received about a letter a day since she left. All unopened—untouched. Having to relive her decision over and over again through letters sounded too painful for me. Knowing that she chose him—Parker, over me was enough. But knowing and having to be reminded again and again that she would never be mine would only make me suffer more. The wound was still fresh; I needed time to heal.

I grabbed my cell phone and swiped my finger across the screen, unlocking it. I had been cancelling all of my clients for the past couple of weeks...not trusting myself around the female population. I knew exactly what my habits were after a bad break-up. Get wasted— forget—rebound. But losing Maddy had left me hollow. Nothing seemed appealing anymore. It's funny how that works...I was going along with my life just fine, happy even, and then she sat down next to me—and everything changed. It's amazing how one small moment can change your life in ways you never thought possible.

I had no intention of taking on clients again until I was one hundred percent. But even that didn't stop me from attempting total self-destruction. Since Maddy had left, my friend and neighbor, Elijah had been dragging me along to bars and parties with him trying to get me out of my funk. It was more awkward than anything...I pushed away the women by being a complete asshole and pissing Eli off.

The only thing that has really kept me going in this time is when I day dream about my next destination; when I fantasize about leaving and starting again fresh. I had been researching for a few days and two destinations had caught my eye; Tahiti and Croatia. I would be content with either, I'm sure, but I was looking for a place to help me forget...help me forget *her*.

Two – A Necessary Change

Jacqueline

It had been over three months since I had last spoken to Parker; since he had called me from Hawaii for advice. Not that he hadn't been reaching out—just that I hadn't been taking his calls. Oddly enough, letters began arriving from Madalynne...the girl he had chosen over me. I wasn't sure what to expect out of them so I let them pile up for weeks. Until one night it was like the pile was glaring at me and I couldn't ignore them anymore. I ended up devouring the letters in one sitting.

I wasn't sure how I was supposed to feel about the letters, but after the third one I found myself laughing and crying with the tales she told. She apologized for her feelings towards me even though I had never known about them. She apologized for what Parker had put me through when he gave me hope and then pulled away. She wrote about her experience with Lee and how much he had changed her life.

Then, something happened that I wasn't expecting. I grew fond of her letters. I found myself waiting impatiently at the door every single day to see if a new one would come. Originally she had sent one a week. But when I had failed to reply they became more distant...fewer and far between. By the sixth letter I had broken down and written her back. It was nearly impossible for me to hate her after she had opened herself up to me so fully. I came to admire her; respect her.

A friendship began to blossom and we were corresponding not only by letters, but by emails and calls too. I came to lean on her for advice. She was the first ever real friend I had that wasn't a guy. I wanted to cherish the relationship.

"Oh, Travis is here, I have to go," I mumbled into my cell phone as he approached. Madalynne had called nearly two hours earlier and we had gotten caught up talking.

"You too," I replied to Madalynne before hanging up.

"Let me guess...Maddy?" Travis said, sarcastically, already knowing the answer.

His brown eyes twinkled as he laughed when I stuck my tongue out at him.

17

"If I didn't know any better, I'd think you have a girl crush on her," he teased, ruffling my blond hair playfully.

"Hey, stop!" I pushed him away, not being able to feign a smile. Travis knew me better than anyone. I could hang out with him every day of the week and never get tired of him. A part of me had always loved him…but as a brother. Luckily, he never passed that imaginary line so I never had to face that awkward moment.

"So, what's on the agenda?" He asked as he slid his fingers through his short blond mane. "And what in the world are you wearing?"

I looked down at my outfit. He was right. I looked the definition of homely with my two sweaters, sweatpants, and jacket, but to be fair it had been excruciatingly cold the past few weeks, being November. "It's freezing outside!" I whined.

He looked at me like I had two heads. "That does not excuse your choice in outfit." He chuckled.

"Oh shut up!" I replied, huffily.

"Well, what kind of trouble do you want to get into?" He looked down at me. Travis was over six feet tall. Anytime I stood beside him, I felt like he towered over me.

"I kind of just want to lay low tonight." It was true. Travis had been dragging me out along with his friends the past few weekends and while it was fun for the first half, I always felt unstable and ready to go home much earlier than anticipated. Plus, most of his friends couldn't stand me. Travis tried to hide that fact, but I could see it in their eyes when they looked at me. They always thought he could do better than a friend like me. Luckily Travis didn't buy into the bullshit. He always made his own decisions, especially when it came to me. That's what I loved about him.

"Walking Dead and snacks?" He offered up. It was our favorite pastime when we stayed in. We would have Walking Dead marathons and stuff ourselves silly with too much sugar and salt.

I nodded, wiggling my eyebrows at him. "Now you're talking my language."

"I'll get the car!" He tossed over his shoulder as he ran out of my apartment. It had been near freezing the past couple of weeks being

19

November, so I was grateful I didn't have to make the long hike to the visitor's parking space with him.

He's going to make someone very happy someday. So why did I feel so guilty that I didn't see him that way?

I've been in foster care for three months and already been through three different homes. No one can handle my frequent outbursts. They all just pass me on like I meant nothing to begin with. So, I'm not normal...who is these days? I saw my mother the other day. It wasn't much of a surprise—she was working her usual corner. She begged for money and when I didn't have any basically discarded me like I was yesterday's trash. She's not a mother...she's a monster.

Every day I sit outside my school waiting for the bus...observing life passing me by. My heart hurts when I catch sight of the loving mothers who come to pick up their children...when I hear stories of what they did for their children.

I know I'm a handful, and I know I'm not easy to deal with, but I just wish for once I meant something to anyone...anywhere. It's the loneliest feeling in the world being shoveled between homes and having no real source of stability, no real time to build relationships or bond. I just wish someone loved me. I just wish I wasn't so easily tossed aside.

Lee

I've been in Belize for nearly two weeks. It's been incredible, but still I find myself bored. I've had a few hook-ups here and there, but no girl has really even intrigued me. I'm a guy and I'm horny, so it looks like tonight will be another one of those mindless nights of sex.

Some nights when I'm alone with my thoughts I toy with the idea of finding one girl to settle down with; one girl to give myself to fully. But then I think about Taylor and as quick as I let the idea in, I shove it out without further attention. Taylor was the only girl I ever dated exclusively—the only girl I ever gave my heart to. I thought the sun rose with Taylor and the moon set with her. I was only seventeen years old when I met Taylor Jacks.

I fell in love with her instantly. Whether it was her contagious laugh or her emerald green eyes—she captivated my soul. We were inseparable for nearly two years before she was cruelly ripped away from me. I remember the phone call. It was my 19th birthday and my birthday was ruined every year with the memory from that day on.

"Hello?"

"Lee?" It was Taylor's sister…she was hysterical. I could tell she was hyperventilating and crying and she couldn't form full sentences.

"Jess? Is that you? Are you okay?" My heart began beating out of my chest; my mind racing.

She continued to sob incoherently and I knew in that moment nothing was ever going to be the same again. "Taylor?" I asked, positive I didn't want to hear the answer.

Just the mention of her sister's name threw Jessica into another round of sobs. My eyes were darting all around my room. I could feel the emotion building inside me. "She's gone isn't she?" The minute I said the words aloud I cracked. I threw up after a few moments of letting the idea of her being gone forever sink into my soul; my core.

I shut down entirely after I lost her. I couldn't bear the thought of moving on with my life and her not being a huge part of it. The beginning of our entire college experience had been alongside one another. She was my pillar of support; my rock. I couldn't imagine ever letting anyone else as close as Taylor had been in fear of losing them. Losing Taylor had nearly been my destruction. If I ever had to face that feeling again—it would be my annihilation.

No strings attached sex seemed like the easiest route. Yet it was anything but. Feelings always got involved no matter how many rules you set before jumping into bed. My hook-ups almost always wanted more from me…something I wasn't entirely ready to give.

It's been over two years since I lost her. But I'm still reminded by her daily; subtle little things. There's one thing I haven't been able to do since she passed— blondes. It doesn't matter if they look nothing like her and resemble a rabbit…blondes are too much for me. Brunettes, black, and red heads are enough of a change I can give a good performance and then never talk to them again.

I've been checking out this brunette beauty the past few days; scoping her out—seeing her personality. She's the bartender at my hotel and we've spent the past few nights chit chatting until the wee hours of the morning. I know I need to seal the deal soon if I don't want to risk her getting attached.

I'm at the bar and she has refilled my drink twice. Now is as good a time as any to go in for the kill. "What do you have planned tonight after you get off?"

She comes closer to the bar and leans her palms on it, flirtatiously. "I thought you'd never ask."

I grin back at her. Her name is Sonia and her brown eyes and long, sleek black hair suit her perfectly. Her accent turns me on. The way she rolls her r's. I let my

23

mind wander to what else she could do with that tongue vibration. It's difficult not to.

"Ten thirty," she mouths back at me as she pours a shot of whiskey for a fellow patron.

"I'll be here," I whisper back before downing my drink and heading back to my hotel. After a few hours have passed I've made my way back to the bar, it's hopping at this time of night. It's definitely a sight to see...the bar is right on the sand of the beach and with all the lights that are strung, the illuminations are beautiful.

Sonia catches sight of me and I watch as her lips curl up in a mischievous smile. It doesn't take rocket scientist to figure out what is on her mind. I lick my lips hungrily, wondering how much longer she is going to make me suffer. I literally eye-fuck her until she gets beet red in the face. "I'm getting off now, stop it."

I smile back, baring my pearly whites at her. I'm charming and I know it. Sonia looks flustered; running a hand through her silky black hair.

No more than ten minutes later and I already had her shirt off and her panting heavily. "Oh Lee," she moans as I kiss and lick her ear delicately. It's making me harder by the minute. I can feel the blood rushing to my member. This high; even for the short lived time, makes it all worth it.

We hadn't even made it back to my hotel room. In fact, I had her pressed up against the back of her bar; back by the dumpsters. It wasn't the ideal place, but neither of us wanted to wait. She was facing the bar, in her bra and jeans and I was pressed up against the back of her; my mouth and hot breaths tickling her neck and ear. "I want you," I whisper into her ear. I felt her shudder with this.

"Not here," I hear her say faintly, shifting so she was now facing me. She kissed me eagerly then—I tasted a strange mix of peppermint and vodka.

At this point, I was willing to follow her anywhere. "Lead the way princess."

I don't know what changed my mind. I don't know when I finally made the decision to open Maddy's letters, but I was glad I did. What I had feared the most had actually given me the strength and courage to move on. Plus she gave me answers to questions I had been holding deep inside myself. Without even realizing it, I had begun to write Maddy back…one letter at first…and then our correspondence grew.

I let myself enjoy the familiarity I got from her letters, but had to keep reminding myself that nothing was ever going to be the same with me and Maddy. We were building a new friendship, and I was simply happy for that.

After writing Maddy for over a month, she brought up Jacqueline for the first time.

The girl I had once cared so deeply about was trying to set me up with a mutual friend of hers and Parker's. The situation was all kind of strange. Maddy said there was something different about Jacqueline and that I should get over my fear of online dating and give her a chance. I won't lie and say it wasn't intriguing. Madalynne mentioned she was blond...and I instantly put my wall up.

Just give her a chance. Madalynne told me once in one of her letters. *I don't know what happened to you in your past, but Jacqueline has had a really tough one. Don't judge her by yours—she isn't judging you on yours.* She had a point. I had been avoiding blondes like the plague, but maybe I was being too harsh. Maybe because of my selectiveness I was losing out on potential love.

After close to a month of poking and prodding; Madalynne finally got her way. I sent Jacqueline a Facebook message asking if she might be interested in chatting. For some reason I had butterflies in the pit of my stomach. It was so unlike me. Deep down though, knowing that Madalynne spoke highly of Jacqueline—I wanted to impress her just as badly. In a way I wanted Jacqueline to run back to Maddy and tell her how much of a catch I was and how she really messed up. It was a pipe dream, but one I clung to with everything in me. It was really all I had left these days—hope.

The last letter I received from Maddy asked me to be a witness at the courthouse for her upcoming nuptials to Parker. The idea made me sick to my stomach. Marriage really puts things into perspective. I knew it wouldn't be for another ten months, but getting used to the idea was going to take a bit of time. Secretly, I think that's why Maddy told me so early, without holding back the information. She wanted to let it sink in; let me digest it. If it were any other way I would have declined the invitation immediately.

I decided a mental break was much needed. After pulling out nearly a thousand dollars from savings, I booked a last minute trip to Berkley, California. I needed out. I needed a change.

Three – Friend Requests & Flirts

Jacqueline

I remember the first close call like it was yesterday. The blood dripping down the back of my leg, Travis's wide eyes, and my stammering response, "I-I accidentally nicked myself."

He never pushed the issue. He didn't ask more questions; just rushed to my side, applying pressure via toilet paper to my wound. I know he saw the scars.

We never spoke about it—we still don't speak about it. It was awkward enough being caught red handed, so we simply continued on with life as normal as we could.

Another topic we avoid? My disorder. In fact, we dance around the conversation all together. Travis is too much of a softy when it comes to me and always lets my mistakes slide—even when he shouldn't.

I was lurking around on Facebook, bored out of my mind when a notification popped up. It was a new friend request.

I clicked on the highlighted symbol and was surprised when a handsome male's photo was staring back at me.

He had brown skin and shaved black hair. He looked like he might be Filipino. Or maybe even Mexican? His name was Lee Bennett. The name sounded so familiar, but I just couldn't put my finger on it. Then I clicked on his picture and his profile popped up on my screen.

I glanced quickly at our mutual friends. We shared two—Madalynne Johnson and Parker Grant. *It can't be...*

I was still lost in my shock when an IM popped up on my screen startling me.

You really going to leave me hanging like that? Sweating? It was from Lee—I assumed, regarding his unapproved friend request.

I wondered what Madalynne and Parker must have told Lee to push him to find me on Facebook. *Do I know you?* I typed back, but added in a wink face emoticon before pressing send.

Har Har Har, he shot back almost instantly, causing my lips to curve up into a slight smile.

Hi, my name is Recently Heartbroken—and you are? He sent after being met with silence on my end.

I laughed a small chuckle before instantly feeling bad. Lee had been the other guy—the one on the side; just like I had been the other girl. We had a lot more in common than I originally thought. *Nice to meet you Recently Broken. I'm Fractured.*

He had a quick wit and had almost instantly sent back a response. *Seems like we have a lot of things in common, Fractured. Unfortunately, they weren't happy experiences. My friend suggested we get to know one another. She implied we might get along.*

I was still giggling. *Can we talk normal yet?*

Thank God. It's almost as if I could hear the breath release in his response.

So Maddy thinks we would get along? I guess we better trust her—she seems to always be spot on. I knew I couldn't sit and chat with Lee all day as I needed to go grocery shopping, but I found myself awaiting a response; completely intrigued.

I'm down if you are tiger, he shot back finally.

Butterflies began fluttering around in my stomach. Attraction was never going to be an issue—Maddy and I tended to have the same taste when it came to that, but letting him in, letting him close was what terrified me most. Being let down is the worst feeling in the world, but his demeanor and quick wit made me want to throw all my inhibitions out the window, and against my better judgment, I found myself opening up to the possibility—but only slightly.

Lee

"Better quit that, or people will think we are together!" Austyn pushes me playfully away from her.

"What? You don't find this attractive?" I joke lightheartedly back.

Her copper eyes widen as her lips curl unwillingly into a tight smile. "You're disgusting, you know that?" She turns her head away from me, her black bob slightly dancing with the turn.

A week ago I had an itch to get out of the city and do something spontaneous so I called up my cousin Austyn and was ecstatic when she agreed to come. We had been tight as thieves since we were kids. She is the same age as me, our birthdays are only days apart. She is more like my best friend; my sister. We tell each other everything and have always been there for one another...she had been best friends with Taylor too.

Austyn is in college so I knew it would be nice to get her out of school and do something unexpected for her, so I paid for the entire trip for the both of us. We are both ready to party and explore our new home for the next week. Our destination? The Bahamas. We had packed and hidden quite well, a few flasks of alcohol, and we knew by the time we were in the Bahamas, it would be legal for us to consume it.

"Don't look now, but I think someone has the hots for you," I whisper into Austyn's ear.

Her eyes light up with fascination. "Where?"

"Don't make it obvious or anything," I joke, laughing lightly.

She elbows me in the chest, smiling.

I back up, hands in the air, surrendering. "I'm just being a good wing man."

"Seriously." Her eyes shoot around the room, nervously. "Which one was it?"

I grin to myself. I love messing with her. I can basically see the sweat beads forming at the tip of her forehead. I try to stifle my laugh, but am unsuccessful.

"You're an ass, you know that, right?" She turns away from me angrily and begins walking towards the inside cabins.

I grab her arm quickly, stopping her mid-step. "He's going to be too intimidated with me standing here with you. I'm going to go back to the room, and why don't you invite him back—we can drink and get to know him in a laid back atmosphere."

She looks me in the eyes then, her copper eyes bearing into my soul. "Which one?"

I love that she is always up for a challenge. "Skater boy," I reply before turning away and making my way back towards our room.

It doesn't take her long. I didn't think it would. Austyn is undoubtedly gorgeous. Guys fall over her all the time. The funny thing is, she never realizes it. She has this odd self-confidence issue. I'm not sure where it stems from or why she is still so affected by it, but it is the reason she is still single today. It is the reason she is always getting hurt. The guys she dated in the past walked all over her like she was nothing but a dirty rug. I think it tore her down. I wish she saw what I saw, when she walked in a room. She is like a magnet—all eyes lock on her. She has no idea that she is a star.

Skater boy is surprisingly really cool. We have a lot in common and he brought a housewarming gift. Austyn is sweet; she gets flustered when illegal activities are occurring, yet, you can tell she wants to partake, always. He lights up the joint, takes a puff and then passes it to me. I can see Austyn's face reddening by the minute; I notice the awkward jerking movement of her leg. "What's your name man?" I ask, attempting to pull his attention off of her.

"Avery," he responds, running his hand through his shaggy long hair.

I finish my hit and then motion for Austyn to come take one. Her eyes are shifting between me and the joint nervously. I nod my head lightly; it always seems to calm her down. She scoots closer to me and takes the rolled piece from my hands, like she is an expert; sucking in the smoke, holding it, and then letting it out in one long breath. She doesn't even cough, which makes me give her a mental high five with my eyebrows. I can see a smile forming at the sides of her lips and I nudge her lightly with my elbow.

"I'm Lee, and you've already met Austyn." I point to her and hand him back his gift.

"Excuse me," Austyn gets up quickly, heading to the bathroom. I watch her walk away and then revert my attention back to Avery.

"So…are you two, like, together?" He finally asks. I have to stop myself from laughing; Austyn had been right for once.

"She's my cousin dude," I smile, shaking my head.

Avery looks relieved. I notice his chest fall like he had breathed out a sigh he had been holding in.

"Does she have a boyfriend?" Avery asks, passing me the joint.

I wave my hands in front of my body as if to say I'm good. "Do you think I would let her be here with you, if she did?"

"Oh, I guess not..." He laughs awkwardly, before putting the joint out.

Four – Challenge Accepted

Lee

Berkley, California was exactly what the doctor ordered. I had only been in town for two days and my cousin and best friend had managed to keep me busy and my mind off of Madalynne. In fact, we had been on the go since I stepped foot off the plane; I hadn't even had a moment to think about anything really.

Austyn knew me too well. She knew my triggers and how easily I could turn on my self-destruction switch, and somehow she always managed to keep me at bay when I needed it most. She has this nurturing way of bringing me back down and reminding me what's important.

Avery, Austyn's boyfriend of a year has been awesome as well. I knew we were going to be great friends the first day we met him on our cruise to the Bahamas. And I was happy to see someone *worthy* of my cousin step up to the plate. I was tired of her being walked all over and hurt.

Austyn and Avery were my two most favorite people in the world to spend time with. They were so much fun and adventurous, like me; I never knew what they had planned next.

"You hungry, man?" Avery turned to me, his long shaggy brown hair obstructing part of his view.

I nodded. "Yeah, actually."

"What are you hungry for?" I heard Austyn's voice chime in from the living room. I had forgotten about her supersonic hearing.

"You know, I could really go for some Middle Eastern food right now," I admitted. My mind was already filling up with images of kabobs and hummus. My stomach began to rumble. I guess I hadn't realized just how famished I was.

"Austyn and I go to this Persian restaurant down the street called Cyprus, it's really good. It's only a couple of blocks down," Avery offered up. I could see him contemplating his order already.

I nodded instantly. Unbeknownst to Avery, I had dated a Persian girl in high school and had fallen in love with their culture and food. "Let's go!"

We wasted no time heading to the restaurant.

I was beginning to see more and more firsthand what I wanted my next relationship to be like. Austyn and Avery were so kind to each other, so gentle. And I had yet to witness a fight, but Austyn had informed me multiple times before, in conversation, that Avery didn't believe in fighting or confrontation. Austyn said he believed in a resolution by words. I envied him for that. I was known to be a bit of a hot head; especially during arguments and I wished that I had the kind of restraint to hold back—cool down—and simply talk things out.

"How do you guys feel about blind dates?"

"Do you have a blind date?" Austyn's eyes shot up, in fascination.

I laughed at her reaction. It wasn't really a blind date, but I had no idea what to call it. A blind set up? That didn't really fit either. "Not necessarily," I found myself saying.

"Spill." Austyn stared me down—her copper eyes fixated on nothing but my lips.

I couldn't help but crack a smile. "It's complicated."

Avery was now piercing me with his stare. "Give us the Cliff Notes version."

Where do I even begin?

"Madalynne," I began before Austyn rudely interrupted me by waving her arms madly.

"I thought this trip was to get over Madalynne—not to dredge up old feelings."

"It is," I replied, honestly.

"Then why are we hearing her name?" She asked, curiously.

"She wants to set me up with a friend of hers...well, hers and Parker's..." I trailed off, knowing how crazy it must sound. Damn, it sounded insane to me just relaying it back.

"Wait—wait—wait." Austyn shook her hand in front of my face wildly. "You're telling me that the girl that broke your heart wants to set you up with a friend of hers, who is also coincidentally friends with the guy she chose over you?"

I nodded, remaining mute.

"And what's holding you back?" Her question threw me off guard. It was not one I had been prepared for in the least.

"You think this is a good idea?" I shifted my eyes between my boisterous cousin and her boyfriend who had been suspiciously quiet during our whole interaction.

Avery spoke then, "You're the one who is always preaching to us about taking risks, not looking back, reaping the rewards. Right? So what in the world would stop you from accepting this challenge?" His advice was spot on. He was right. When had I ever been afraid?

"And plus, you deserve to be happy," Austyn said softly, squeezing my shoulder.

I smiled back at them. "I'd like that."

Jacqueline

"Show me," she says, eyeing me sternly.

Yeah, right.

"You wanted my help right?" Ms. Brown asks. "Well in order for that to happen I need to know how deep you are in this."

Ms. Brown, or as she likes to be called Kim is the youngest therapist I have ever been to. I liked her almost instantly because she could easily relate, but what she's asking is so out of my comfort zone.

"If you don't show me, I have no choice but to release these records to the hospital," she threatens.

I stare in her eyes for a long time, daring her to follow through with her threat. In the end, I'm the one who loses. She has me admitted into Pinecrest. She says it's for my safety.

My admit papers state it is for self-harming and suicide watch. Normally when something this life altering and embarrassing happens you worry about your reputation and what people will think about you.

I don't have that luxury. The only thing I ponder is if Travis will find a way to locate me.

I wake up every morning and chant the same mantra, 'You're not crazy—you just have an addiction you need to get over.'

It works well enough. I've been at Pinecrest for a week and already find myself wondering how I made it so far in life without Lucky.

Lucky has attempted to end her life on three separate occasions, unsuccessfully. She is the butt of many jokes due to her name and the third time's a charm rule not *working. She is familiar with Pinecrest and has been admitted three different times. The rumors are that she just wants attention. I close them out. She has been and is a wonderful mentor for me.*

Lucky reminds me what it feels like to be happy; to feel alive. Always smiling and positive; she opened up to me almost immediately. 'Honey, you remind me so much of myself when I was a young girl.' I can recall her saying.

Five – Silence is Deadly

Jacqueline

My head rolled back, dizziness slowly taking me over.

It had been two days, seven hours, and nineteen minutes since I had last indulged. Not that I was counting or anything, but the release was just what I needed; what I had been craving.

After sitting in silence for fifteen minutes, I made myself get moving. I blotted my leg, and then quickly put a Band-Aid on the back of my leg. I knew it wasn't normal—I worried all the time no one would be able to accept it. I worried one day I would run out of landscape to mess with and when that time came, no one would want me.

I opened the door to my bathroom and walked out, headed to my computer. I glanced at the clock above the desk. I had about an hour and a half before I needed to get ready for work.

I signed into Facebook and was surprised to find another correspondence from Lee. It had been from earlier that morning.

"Hey, you up?" It read. I looked at the time sent—4:42 am. Wow, either he was a night owl or an extreme early bird.

I noticed his picture had a green dot on it—meaning he was still online.

I am now—what's up? I wrote back, curious as to his intentions.

I just got back from the most amazing run, he wrote. *You?*

He was an extremist, alright. *I just woke up,* I shot back, lamely.

Oh, right—it is early there. My bad, Lee replied.

No worries.

So, what are your plans for the day? Lee typed.

Work, unfortunately, I replied.

Where do you work? He seemed very interested in getting to know me and wasn't afraid to show it.

I work for my friend's mom; with horses. I knew how much I loved and enjoyed the work I did, but my explanation just sounded lame.

You work with horses? What an awesome job. His response surprised me.

You like horses?

I love horses. Sometimes I think I was a horse in a past life—running wild and free. Is that weird? His answer made me smile. I had yet to see why Maddy had dumped him…except for the biggest reason of all, Parker.

So, what animal do you think you were in a past life? Lee asked after being met with silence for several minutes.

I thought silently to myself before responding. *I think I was a bird—one that flew high above the trees and looked over the land.*

Who's the weird one now? He placed a silly emoticon at the end of his sentence, hinting at his joke.

You intrigue me, Mr. Bennett, I teased.

Mr. Bennett? Did we take a step backwards? Why are you addressing me so formally? Lee is cool too… I could practically picture a confused smile spreading slowly across his face.

I've been hurt in the past and I'm still picking up the pieces. I have a lot of issues—ones that will make you run the other way. Do you really want to waste your time with someone like me? I had no idea what brought on my sudden case of honesty or why I felt like being so candid with a total stranger, but there was something about Lee, something I couldn't put my finger on. I knew this much—I felt like I could trust him.

Tell me one thing you think will make me run the other way and I will surprise you with my answer. He pushed.

I sat, without typing anything for minutes...there were so many to choose from. I was broken and damaged and Lee had no idea what kind of baggage I carried, but for one reason or another I found myself not able to hold back.

Here goes nothing.

I am bipolar... I typed timidly.

I sent it and then waited.

And waited some more.

Nothing.

I looked at his picture and noticed the green dot was missing notifying me that he was no longer online.

Son of a bitch.

Color me surprised…

Six – Progress Report

Lee

I'm kind of an asshole. I know it. I just hadn't been expecting her to be so open and honest with me. And her disorder? I knew little to nothing about it, so after a night or two of mulling it over, I decided to curb my curiosity by researching it.

Bipolar disorder: *A condition in which a person has periods of depression and periods of being extremely happy or being cross and irritable.*

I sat back—taking it in. It was a bit overwhelming for me. I avoided getting online for days as I let reality sink in. I was so not one for drama…and I loved having a good time and being happy. If I had to worry constantly if my partner was okay or happy and not depressed and irritable, that just seemed like an unnecessary stress I didn't need.

Why can't I just find someone normal?

Not wanting to deal with it as usual, I did what I was best at—avoidance and self-destruction.

Before I even knew what was happening—I was at my favorite dive bar, The Bar to Nowhere, downing my second Fireball shot.

My favorite distraction had always been alcohol and slutty girls...until Maddy. But it seemed like I was having no trouble falling right back into my old patterns when I texted one of my usual hook-ups, Cami, to meet me.

She looked sluttier than usual, if that was even possible. Her skirt barely covered her tight ass and her boobs had come out to play.

Normally I would feel the blood rushing to Willie almost instantly when I caught sight of Cami's strawberry blond hair cascading over her double D's. Her green eyes always held a hint of playfulness. And when she would bite her lip—it would make me all sorts of crazy.

As sexy as Cami had been to me, I also found myself turned off by her. The fact that she tried so hard was unattractive. I was one for the chase—and Cami gave up before the race even began—it was almost too desperate.

She was so high maintenance and I had a feeling she would turn into Medusa and crush my dreams if I ever gave her my heart—I had just seen how much of a malicious person she

49

was and I wanted no part of it...but the sex—the sex was amazing.

"Hey you," she purred as she rubbed the back of my hair with her long fake nails.

Normally she knew that would drive me mad, but something was off tonight. I wasn't horny in the slightest. *Just get laid and forget about today,* the devil on my left was telling me. The angel on my right was saying, *what the hell are you doing here? This isn't what you really want.*

"You want a drink?" I found myself asking instead.

"A vodka cran." She never took her eyes off of me.

I signaled the bartender and watched as he hurried over. "Vodka cran for the lady and another Fireball for me."

"You got it," Todd nodded back at me. I came to this bar enough to know the entire staff and even some of the usual patrons.

If it wasn't already obvious enough—Cami applied the perfume she knew could make me do things without thinking—she was playing the game perfectly tonight.

Normally I wouldn't blink twice before taking her back to my place and ripping all her clothes off—but even the thought of getting laid was a buzz kill tonight.

Todd brought back our drinks and my shot was gone—down the hatch within seconds of clinking our glasses. I was beginning to feel it—the numb feeling I had grown so accustomed to since Taylor. It was the one steady thing in my life I could count on no matter what.

Cami was staring at me expectedly, waiting for me to break the silence and pose the question I always did at this time. But I wasn't feeling it.

"So how have you been?" I found myself asking instead. Small talk seemed like a safe route to take.

The alcohol was doing its job. I could feel it slowly seeping through my body as my bones felt incredibly hot and then numb as usual.

Cami was surprised by the conversation. To be quite honest, I normally never bothered to ask her any questions—I was sure she was having a field day in her mind.

"Good…" she finally replied. I could see her agitation growing by the minute…unfortunately, I was enjoying it.

Just tell her you're not feeling it and dip out. My inner voice had a point, but my legs were feeling like jello.

"Cami…how long have we known each other?" I spoke up again.

"Two years," Cami answered, showing a hint of more interest.

"Two years—and do you know what? I don't even know your last name." It was true. In the two years I had known Cami I hadn't bothered to find out anything about her. And yet, she hadn't gotten the hint yet?

"It's Trammel," she said with a tight smile. I could tell she was growing more irritable by the second.

If there was one thing in the world Cami and I did have in common, it was our love for mind-blowing sex. But nothing, and I repeat, nothing compares to sex with the person you love.

There is added passion and heat; a different type of energy; and even a different type of communication. After experiencing sex with Maddy, I wasn't sure I ever wanted to settle for mind-blowing sex again, when I could have the former.

Cami was staring half-expectedly at me and half-annoyed. And the only thing going through my mind? I wanted to apologize to Jacqueline for signing off without a goodbye after she was so open and honest with me. The one thing I had been so scared of was now the one thing pulling me back towards her like a magnet.

"What are you thinking about?" I heard Cami's soft voice near my ear, her breath tickling me.

"A girl," I replied, honestly.

Cami looked excited for a moment, assuming I was referring to her.

"I don't think we should see each other anymore," I blurted out, then was immediately met with a death glare from hell.

If looks could kill...

She remained silent—just staring me down with that icy stare of hers.

"Go fuck yourself," she finally hissed before proceeding to pour the rest of her drink over my head. "Don't bother calling Bennett; I won't pick up!" She said angrily, calling me by my last name—something she was used to doing in bed, before stomping out loudly.

You deserved that douche bag.

Seven – Leave a Message at the Tone

Jacqueline

Tonight was not a good night for me. Honesty was overrated. All I could think of was how I scared away the one guy I had seen potential in since Parker, and had probably ruined my chances. Who would want to be with a broken bipolar freak like me anyways?

My depression was kicking my ass and I felt like I had been run over by a train.

I spent over an hour attempting to curl my hair as a way to cheer myself up, but when the curls became difficult I threw the iron at the mirror; shattering it into a million pieces—bad luck, I've heard.

I couldn't trust myself tonight and some online distractions sounded like exactly what I needed.

Not expecting anything when I signed into Facebook, my breath caught in my throat from a message in my inbox from Lee.

My emotions were all over the place. I wanted to strangle him—I wanted to find out why—but most of all, I was curious.

I opened the message against my better judgment.

I'm an ass—I'm sorry. Forgive me?

It was short and sweet and to the point. I found myself smiling, but then remembered how he had been making me feel the past few days.

Yeah you are.

It seemed simple enough, until I noticed that Lee was online and my heart rate spiked again. I could tell he was already writing back.

Tell me how much of an asshole I am over the phone. 808-337-4986.

He was making my blood boil. *You're not ready for that.*

Try me, he replied.

I almost felt bad for him. If he even saw what I had done to my mirror, he would have run the other way. But I wasn't one to break away from a challenge, so before I even processed what I was doing—I was dialing the number he had given me.

"Whoa, I didn't expect you to actually call me. I figured you would text—but hi," he answered in one long breath. His voice was sexy and mysterious, but I couldn't forget why I had bothered to make the phone call in the first place.

"You're an ass," I blurted into the phone. Somehow, it didn't make me feel any better.

"We've established this already. You sound sexy when you're mad," Lee replied; which only fueled my rage more. Was he making fun of me?

"I think I'm going to go before I say something I'm going to regret," I began to hang up the phone when I heard Lee interject.

"Awww, but where would be the fun in that?" He asked in a low voice.

This boy was driving me crazy. "Is everything a joke to you?" I asked dryly.

"No Mrs. Serious Pants—but would it kill you to lighten up?" He was pushing my buttons— one more push—and I wasn't going to be able to contain my anger and frustration—I was going to go postal on him.

"You're walking a thin line—better check yourself," I said through gritted teeth.

"Before I wreck myself?" Lee asked, and I could clearly picture the grin plastered across his face as he delivered that line.

He was met with a disconnection.

Eight – Surprises and Sucker Punches

Lee

"It feels like we haven't seen you in forever man," Avery releases me from his hug so Austyn can take her turn at me.

She practically topples me over as she jumps on me and gives me the tightest hug ever. I can't help but chuckling. "I missed you too."

I have been traveling almost non-stop since the cruise where Austyn met Avery—and while they've spent almost every waking moment together since, and their relationship has only blossomed...I've made sure not to stop moving. When I do, I am forced to remember that I can't have my happy ending like that. Taylor is not here to enjoy it with me. I wonder when the day will come when she doesn't cross my mind a million times or where I don't picture her face before I go to bed at night.

"We've been worried about you," Austyn says softly.

I scoff loudly and obnoxiously, "you're worried about me? Tell me little cousin, what has got you so riled up?"

"Have you been drinking?" Her eyes squint as she tries to make the assessment of me.

I had. On the plane I had managed to flirt my way into three complimentary travel bottles of vodka. I made sure they didn't go to waste. I might have joined the mile high club with the stewardess who had snuck them to me...but I was not telling.

Austyn has somehow managed to inch closer to me, inhaling my breath. "Oh my God, you are drunk!"

I roll my eyes. "And you're overreacting mother.

Austyn glares back at me. "Don't play the asshole Lee, leave it to the experienced."

It is like a punch in the gut to hear her say this.

"We're worried about your drinking." It is Avery who speaks now, but his voice stays low and calm.

"Why?" I press. "Because I have the occasional beer with dinner? Whoopty-doo."

"It's more like a case of beer with dinner," Austyn says gently.

"I'm a drunk—so what?" I want nothing more than to shut the conversation down altogether.

"You need help Lee," Austyn continues, "You're an alcoholic."

I shoot a glare in her direction. I can't believe she just went there. "I'm out of here!" I reply huffily, grabbing my jacket off the back of the chair.

"Don't you ever want to settle down Lee? Start a family...fall in love?" The way she asks the questions make it seem like I had never fallen in love the first time. Like Taylor's entire existence was a lie. It breaks my heart.

"I found love—and it was stolen away from me," I hiss through gritted teeth.

"Look man, she is only trying to help," Avery takes a stand between us.

"Well you can tell her to mind her own business—in fact, why don't you heed that advice as well?" My words feel like venom as I spit them at my cousin and best friend.

"Don't do this Lee, you know we didn't mean any harm," Avery warns me, still calm during the storm.

"Too late," is all I get out as I slam their front door and walk out into the snow.

I had been thinking about Jacqueline a lot since she hung up on me. I didn't know what it was, but there was something about her feistiness that drew me in like a magnet.

I loved that she was unpredictable. I loved the fact that she would keep me on my toes. I felt like being spontaneous and enduring the consequences later, so I booked a last minute flight to Montana.

I had every intention on discussing the idea with Jacqueline—but before I knew it, I was at the airport, backpack in tow.

When my feet hit the ground in Montana I dialed her number.

No answer.

I deserved that. I did. I dialed it again, anxiously, hoping she didn't look at me as some kind of desperate freak.

Still no answer.

I decided to resort to texts. *I'm in Montana— surprise.*

She responded within seconds. *Um what?*

I figured an apology in person was necessary. It seemed like the most foolproof way to get her to agree to meet me.

Are you insane? She asked.

I surely hope not, I joked back.

You really hopped a flight to Montana to apologize for being an ass?

Yes?

Her answer took me by surprise. *Well you certainly get brownie points for the stunt.*

I smiled to myself, excited she wasn't going to continue snubbing me. *So you going to come pick me up or leave me stranded at the airport all by my lonesome?*

Do you have a place to stay? She asked, without bothering to answer my previous question.

I'm not completely inept, I responded. *I booked a hotel room.*

How long are you planning on staying?

Could you just cool it with the questions and come pick me up? Or are you stalling for other reasons? I could imagine her cheeks turning a rosy pink at this.

Be there in twenty; and she wasn't kidding; no later than twenty minutes after our texting session had ceased and I could see her walking up to me through the crowd of people.

Her blue eyes and blond hair stunned me to silence for a moment. I broke into a wide grin, unable to contain myself. She was better looking in person than I had pictured. She was wearing a red peacoat and brown leggings paired with tan cowgirl boots. Her straight, long blond hair cascaded over her shoulders effortlessly.

"Jacqueline?" I asked, even though there was no doubt in my mind that it was her.

"You can call me Jacquie you know," she giggled nervously.

"Jacquie, I'm Lee and I'm a recovering ass." I took her soft, delicate hand in mine and kissed it gently.

She chuckled some more. Seeing her smile was enough for me. It made my trip worthwhile.

I don't know what came over me. Like I said she was a magnet and before I could stop myself I had mashed my lips to hers. I felt her surprise, then a moment of reprieve. The warm and fuzzy feeling I instantly felt throughout my body was numbed when I felt her rip her lips away from mine and deck me right across the jaw.

Could you fault me for trying?

Nine – A Bet Lost

Jacqueline

"What the hell do you think you're doing?" I asked, incredulously.

To be honest, it hadn't angered me in the slightest. It had just taken me off guard. In fact, I was positive Lee noticed me begin to kiss him back. But he had no right to be kissing me like that. We knew hardly anything about one another and I felt like he thought I was easy.

I mean, how many other girls had fallen for his smooth ways?

He rubbed his jaw, his facial expression a mix of shock and amusement; his hazel eyes shining even brighter. "You have one hell of a right hook."

I couldn't help but laugh. He looked so innocent, so powerless in the moment. I broke out into a round of chuckles. "Come on Smooth Operator, I'm going to show you where I live." And with that I turned on my heel—leaving him wide-eyed and open mouthed behind me.

When we were both buckled in and on the road, Lee broke the silence. "You're like the craziest girl I've ever met." My heart dropped into my stomach.

This was it—he hadn't even set foot in my state for longer than thirty minutes and I had already scared him off. I was really some kind of freak.

I slammed on my breaks, causing Lee's body to jerk forward. He put his hands up to stop himself from flying into the dashboard. "Just rip it off." Was all I said as I stared at him, unable to move.

His eyes got wide when he saw the lights of cars behind us. They were honking, swerving, cussing, and passing us. "Are you really going to sit here—in the middle of the road? You're going to get us killed!" There was real fear in his voice and it was enough to feel validated.

"If you're going to break up with me—you should just do it now. Get it over with." I looked him in the eyes this time.

"What? We're not even dating…" Was all he could muster up in response. He was still nervously watching the commotion in the side view mirror.

I had created quite the pile-up. Cars were flashing their brights, honking, and motioning me to get off the road.

I stifled a laugh and floored it out of there.

"You're insane," Lee said again, only this time it was in a low whisper.

I tore my eyes off the road to meet his and playfulness and mystery danced across them. I might have been hallucinating, but I think I also saw Lee turned on. He kept biting his lip, and running his hand over his fuzzy shaved head.

"Pull over."

"What?" I asked, puzzled as to what his motives were.

"Pull over," he repeated in the exact same tone and I kid you not—I had never been more turned on in my life.

Before I knew it, I had taken his advice and we were parked outside a local park I used to frequent. It was late, around eight at night and it was dark; not pitch dark though. There were no patrons around. I put the car in park and was sure my heartbeat could be heard across the world.

Lee unbuckled his seatbelt when I parked and shifted in his seat to face me. "I'm not going to kiss you again until you ask for it."

I looked at him, my jaw down to my knees. "What makes you think I would let you kiss me again?" It was all I had been fantasizing about since he had stolen the first kiss from me. It consumed my every thought. But I was not going to tell him that. I was going to remain strong.

"Oh, when I'm done with you—you're going to be begging for it," he said in the cockiest tone I had ever heard.

"Cocky much?" I asked, snidely.

"Confident," Lee responded calmly, grinning back at me.

And then I could feel his warm breath in the crook of my neck, just below my ear, dancing on my skin. My breathing became shallow, and I wondered how he knew where my spot was instantly and the crazy things it would do to me.

If his lips or tongue made their way anywhere towards my neck I was a goner for sure.

I was holding my own. My poker face had not wavered, but my madly beating heart and breathing were a dead giveaway.

"How ya doing over there?" Lee whispered in my ear.

"I'm fine, absolutely fine," I gulped out, attempting to sound confident.

That's when his lips found the bottom of my ear and he kissed it and gently sucked on it, causing me to nearly bite my tongue off as I squealed with pleasure.

"What was that?" Lee asked, putting his ear to my mouth. His neck was irresistibly close and all I could smell was his intoxicating scent—a mix of his cologne and pure pheromones.

Lee backed up again and began nibbling my right ear. Was it getting hot in here? Or was it just me…

Thankfully he hadn't messed with my deadly spot since he began his treacherous reign on my body. I would probably leave horny as hell—but a winner nonetheless.

I wondered if Lee was finding any pleasure at all from his torture raid on me and my body—

but I could tell from his smile and chuckles that he was enjoying himself far too much.

"Still don't want to kiss me?" Lee puckered his lips animatedly.

"Eww! I'd rather kiss a frog!" I made a stink face, pulling away from him, half-heartedly.

"Now you're asking for it!" Lee squealed, heading straight for my neck. At first he was simply trailing it with his breath, close enough to drive me wild, yet not touching me. My whole body stiffened; my senses heightened. It was like he had found the jackpot. Winner winner, chicken dinner.

He didn't waste any time trailing it with his fingers lightly in amazement, how my body twitched and jerked from the simple touch.

He pressed his lips to my neck and I melted into him, breathing increasing, eyes fluttering shut.

I moaned loudly as his tongue slid up and down the base of my neck—my whole body was shuddering, my heart rate was off the charts, and my breathing almost to hyperventilating. I wanted nothing more than to feel his lips on mine again. To feel the roughness they had—the passion.

71

Then I felt his warm breath on my ear again. "You're crazy, Jacqueline."

I looked at him with fire in his eyes.

"Straight up nut job," he smiled.

I sat up straighter, getting more heated by the moment.

"But that's what makes you so damn irresistible." He ran his finger across my lips slowly, delicately, licking his own at the same time. He was staring at my lips—I was transfixed upon his.

Shit.

I guess this means I lost.

Ten – A Dangerous Rendezvous

Lee

I don't know what overcame me. There was something about her. Her feistiness was sexy as hell. I could already tell there was going to be passion—off the charts. Jacqueline was going to keep me on my toes. And I was down for all of it.

She was sitting there, eyes closed, waiting for our lips to meet—but she was stubborn. Not wanting to admit she lost. Our lips were seconds from touching, but I had no plans on leaning in. I was going to have her eating out of the palm of my hand. Maybe I could win Jacqueline's heart in the process.

I could feel her tender breath on my lips as I ran my fingers gently through her blond hair. I rubbed the bottom of her ear softly.

I could feel her shaking and stirring against my touch. It couldn't be much longer until she surrendered to the inevitable closeness.

"Lee," she whispered seductively and the way my name rolled off her tongue had all the blood rushing to my member.

I wasn't sure who made the first move—but our lips were suddenly entangled with one another's, her tongue searching my mouth eagerly.

I heard her moan softly as I tugged on her hair. Our lips were brushing against each other's with urgency. I had my hand tangled in her hair, cupping her face as we went.

She broke off the kiss breathlessly, "whoa."

Whoa was right. She was a phenomenal kisser. She had taken me by complete surprise. I only had one thing on my mind—I was a guy, could you blame me?

I reached over her and unbuckled her seatbelt, pulling the lever to lay her chair back.

"What are you doing?" She asked, still taken aback by my advances.

"Shh." I put my finger on her lip to silence her. Then ran it slowly across the bottom of her lip.

She wasn't expecting it when I climbed on top of her, straddling her. I had one hand cupping her face and the other was entangled within her golden locks. I could feel her pressing into me—into my kisses. She was thrusting her hips towards me, as I was into her.

The passion was increasing by the moment. It was mere moments before her peacoat was ripped off and her tank underneath was pulled over her head. She was left in her bra and leggings. I worried a little that she would be cold, being that it was December, and with the temperatures outside in the low thirties. But there was so much heat emanating off the both of us, we had fogged up all the windows.

She had a lacy zebra print bra and she couldn't have had bigger than size B breasts, but they looked perfect for her size.

I moved my lips from her ear to her neck, which sent her into a round of shivers. It was obvious to anyone that her neck was a spot that could drive her over the edge.

I spent a few minutes torturing her right along her neck and shoulder bones before switching my attention to her chest. I quickly pressed my lips to the part of her breasts that were exposed.

It wasn't long before I had swiftly removed her bra. I took her breast into my mouth, kissing, sucking, and tugging on the nipple softly.

Her moans only grew louder; the blood had rushed all the way to little Lee and he was completely erect through my blue jeans.

It was probably just my imagination, but Jacqueline seemed to press into me closer, rougher. Our thrusting into one another was now completely in sync.

She was shivering and I wasn't sure if it was from the cold outside or the passion. Her breathing had deepened with mine and I wasn't sure I would be able to stop myself.   That was until I heard the loud rapping on the driver's side window.

"Police, open up!"

"License and registration please," the dark haired police officer drones.

I glance up at her, taking in the way her brown eyes compliment her blue uniform. "Sure thing Officer," I answer as I open up the glove box and pull out said registration. I pull my license out of my wallet as well, handing her both pieces. "Can I ask why you pulled me over?"

She stares back at me, annoyed. "Reckless driving, speeding, and your back taillight is out."

I sigh dramatically. "I promise I will slow down from now on and go get my light fixed, how about a warning this time?" I flash her my award winning smile. The same one that has gotten me out of trouble so many times.

She points her flashlight to the inside of my car. I wince knowing full well there are open containers of beer lying around that she is bound to see.

"Sir, have you been drinking tonight?"

I chuckle at the thought of me being called sir. Okay, okay, I'll admit it—I'm a little drunk—but I am maintaining it swimmingly if you ask me. I shake my head as if to say no. "You can call me Lee."

"Well Romeo, I'm going to need you to step out of the car please." She eyes me down. She is shorter and petite. Her black hair cascades down her back, long and full, reaching her rear.

I comply, staggering out of the car. Okay, I'll admit it—I am a bit more wasted than I let on. I raise my hands in surrender as I close my door. "You want to get freaky with those handcuffs?"

My charm is something that has always gotten me out of the worst predicaments. What can I say? I have women eating out of the palm of my hand—and even the sexy officer who pretends to be in shock by my suggestion—shows the slightest hint of intrigue behind her eyes. Yep, it's definitely there.

She recovers quickly enough—but I catch it and I know I am going to win. She puts me through the usual sobriety test before beginning to issue me a citation. She hands it to me and then proceeds to let me know she plans to tow my car.

"You don't want to do this…" I begin as she is tightening the handcuffs around my wrist.

"And why is that?" She asks, giving me the in I so desperately need.

"Because, how will I ever take you on a proper date if I'm locked up? Plus orange really isn't my color."

She blushes with a small smile. I almost have her…just a couple more small pushes and she is bound to be on me like white on rice.

"What's your name?" I ask, as she lowers my head down and helps me into her squad car.

"Officer Dupointe."

I watch as she climbs into the driver's seat and closes her door.

"What's your real name?" I ask, staring at her through the metal bars separating us.

"Taryn." Is all she says.

"Have you ever been in love Taryn? I mean the heart racing, anxiety driven love?" She is backing up the car, on the way to the station.

She nods, remaining mute. I thought so. I could tell she was broken from a mile away. "I was in love once…" I begin, making sure she is engaged in my story before I continue. I catch her eyes in the rearview and know she is in the process of falling under my spell. When I don't immediately continue on with the story she interjects.

"What happened?" There it was. I hooked her. It won't be much longer before I have her hook, line, and sinker.

"She died."

Her eyes glance up in the rearview with guilt. "I-I'm sorry…" she stammers. "What happened?"

"Car accident," I answer simply, staring out the window.

Thinking about Taylor instantly puts me into a sad mood.

Then, out of nowhere, I feel the squad car come to a stop. "What if we forget about this—this one time?"

I can't believe it...it worked.

"Let me take you home. You can pick up your car tomorrow," she says surprising me.

I smile widely back at her. "Now you're speaking my language..."

Eleven – Guilty as Charged

Jacqueline

I was going to kill Lee—I was going to murder him and bury the body.

It was surprisingly my first offense and I was let off with a fine. Lee was not as lucky—turns out he had a bit of a record—it only angered me more.

Lee had some kind of charm—he had somehow manipulated his way out of a short jail stint with a few choice words and his killer smile. I had to admit—he had his ways. He was slapped with a fine like me and we were sent on our way.

"So how about that for a first date?" Lee boasted as we drove away from the officer and the park.

I was seething and couldn't even see straight from the rage. My response was a fresh and strong glare in his direction. I knew if I opened up my mouth it wouldn't be pretty.

"Oh, I get it...you're giving me the silent treatment," he paused for effect. "I guess you're entitled to that this one time."

I glanced over at him, unable to hide my shock—then back at the road—still silent. It was the calmest I had been in days—I was proud of myself.

"Come on, at least admit it...you had fun," Lee whispered, a hint of playfulness dancing behind his eyes.

I tried to fight my smile...but I couldn't help it—if this was the way things were beginning, I could only imagine the rest of his trip.

"See? I knew it!" I wanted to slap the smirk right off his face. This was not what I had signed up for.

"Which hotel are you staying at?" The coolness and indifference in my voice could shatter mirrors.

"So it's going to be like that?" Lee replied in a surprised tone.

"Like what? You almost got us arrested back there...next I'm sure my actual life will be in danger." I didn't bother tearing my eyes off the road that time.

"Oh, come on—Parker always made you seem like such a risk taker," Lee said playfully.

The mention of Parker's name had me going through a whirlwind of emotions.

"You spoke to Parker about me?" I tried to mask the nervousness in my voice. I hadn't taken the necessary time to mourn his absence in my life and wasn't prepared for this.

Too late. Lee's voice sounded dejected. Suddenly, I was kicking myself mentally in the face. I hadn't meant to hurt his feelings. But the fact that he was disappointed at all had to mean something right?

"Yeah, Parker has brought you up a couple of times..." Lee trailed off.

I continued my façade, "oh yeah? Wonder why..." I tried to sound disinterested.

Lee didn't seem to buy it at all. In fact, the couple of times I had stolen glances in his direction, he looked mildly annoyed—staring out the window. "Saddlecreek Inn," he said suddenly.

"Huh?" I found myself asking, my mind still hazy with thoughts of Parker and what if's.

"That's where I'm staying—can you drop me off?"

Shit.

I was transparent and guilty. "I'm sorry," I stammered.

"No, I totally get it—the wound is still fresh. I'm battling a fresh one myself." He smiled lightly back at me, sadness in his eyes.

Now that I finally knew our destination, I found myself taking the long route there.

The route completely out of the way, just to spend a bit more time with him—to clear some of my conscience.

"I forgot how Maddy had kept you in the dark for so long," I said softly. "I'm sorry she did that to you."

"Kept me in the dark?" Lee asked, incredulously. "More like toyed with my emotions—held me by a string, just to cut me loose when she was done with me..."

I had been attempting to smooth things over, but it appeared as though I was just making things worse.

"How much has Maddy told you about me?" I asked.

"That you were blond, cute, and sweet. And that I should get to know you," Lee responded, his body language telling me he was more engaged.

"She didn't tell you anything about my history with Parker?" I glanced over at him just in time to see him shaking his head no.

"We're going to have a lot to talk about over these next few days…" I trailed off as I yet again dodged the street that went to his hotel.

S.O.S.

My heart is racing. S.O.S. is Parker and my emergency signal if anything terrible or unthinkable happens.

We met in an online chat room about suicide—I helped him get through and past his brother's death. In turn it has really brought us close.

We have only been talking for a little over a month now, but it is so unlike Parker to miss a day talking to me. I usually receive a handful of messages all throughout the day, every day.

He is what I look forward to. I don't have internet at my current foster house—so I go to the library for close to four hours every school day. It really is my only means of communication, besides a few phone calls here and there via payphone.

'What's wrong?' I type in response; dying of anticipation.

'Tonight is not a good night for me,' Parker replies almost instantaneously—my heart rate finally slows.

'Don't do anything stupid. You remember how unfair life was after Bo made his selfish choice.'

It isn't really like Parker to do something reckless. He is a goody-goody, always trying to please everyone.

After waiting close to ten minutes for a response, I decide to add something else. 'You can talk to me about anything…you should know that by now.'

'I know.' His response comes fast and quick. 'Why did he have to do it?'

He is referring to his brother Bo. He had committed suicide and Parker had found him. He had been spiraling ever since.

'We'll never know the true answer to that,' I tip-toe around his question. 'But he wouldn't want you feeling *this way. He would want to know you are happy and moving on.'*

'I just don't know any more what there is to move on to.'

I take in a deep breath before responding. 'You have me. Move on to me.'

'I am so thankful I met you.' His sweet compliments always make me swoon.

'Believe me Parker Grant, I think you're going to help me more than I could ever dream of helping you.'

Twelve – Bipolar Freakout

Lee

Even though I had been irritated by Jacqueline's obvious feelings towards Parker, I knew how I felt about Madalynne…I knew how difficult it had been for me to get over her. I wasn't even sure to be honest if I had tackled that feat yet. Plus, I was only in Montana for a few days and I intended to make the best out of my trip.

It was my second day in Missoula, and Jacqueline had managed to get the day off so we could spend some more time getting to know one another. We bundled up because the weather man predicted snow and then I convinced her to take me snowboarding. Turns out she had never been before.

"So wait, you're telling me you've never been snowboarding before?" I asked, staring her down like she had two heads.

She shook her head no.

"What about skiing?" I asked, as we drove to what Jacqueline called "Snowbowl".

Again she remained mute, just shaking her head.

"Sledding?"

She didn't bother acknowledging my question this time. Just looked forward with an uncomfortable, sad expression etched across her face.

Instantly I felt guilty. "Hey," I said lightly, grabbing her left hand in mine. "I'm sorry for pushing."

She glanced at me quickly with a fake smile, then back to the road. "I didn't have the greatest upbringing. I haven't experienced a lot of things—sometimes I feel extremely naïve in this big, bad, world."

"That sounds like a challenge," I replied, my mind racing. "What else haven't you done?"

"That list could go on forever," she laughed uncomfortably.

"Give me a few."

She sighed, exhaling loudly. "Camping, flying, swimming."

I looked back at her, unable to hide my shock.

"I didn't have role models to teach me those things…not to mention I have about one friend in the world." Her response sounded so sad it tugged at my heart strings.

"That's a lie…and you know it. You have at least four friends in this world."

I watched as she rolled her eyes. "Oh, I'm sorry, make that four…they can still be counted on one hand…"

I hadn't realized I was still holding onto her hand. I squeezed it lightly then. "You have so much time."

She nodded, without bothering to respond.

I couldn't imagine my life without adventure, risk, or adrenaline. It saddened me that Jacqueline hadn't been able to experience any of those things I had taken for granted…but I vowed I was going to be the one to change it all.

"Tell me about your family," I said, realizing I knew very little of Jacqueline. Everything had been such a whirlwind I hadn't even stopped for a moment to take it all in. I knew she had kind of dated Parker, lived in Montana, loved horses, was bipolar, and beautiful. But that was about it. "Do you have any siblings?"

"No," she said stiffly. "My mother is in jail and my father skipped out when I was a little girl."

It was all beginning to fall into place. No wonder she hadn't experienced anything in life. "Who do you spend the holidays with?" I asked, knowing Christmas was weeks away.

"My best friend Travis and his family. I've been doing that since I was emancipated."

I inhaled deeply.

"Too much for you to take in?" Jacqueline asked, looking back at me.

I shook my head no before answering. "It's just sad."

"Please don't," Jacqueline said softly.

"What?"

"Please don't feel sorry for me. I've accepted my shitty life and existence and when people

91

begin pitying me it just takes me three steps back."

I swallowed silently. She was more broken than I had anticipated. "Tell me about Travis," I said, hoping to lighten the mood.

"He's been there for me since the beginning. He's seen me at my best and worst and still accepts me. He's the best person I know." The way she spoke about him, and the way her eyes lit up made me worry there was more to their friendship than she let on.

"Have you two ever…" I trailed off, my mind racing with all the possibilities.

She basically scoffed in my face. "Travis and me? No…we're just friends and that's all we've ever been. He's like my brother…"

It eased a little of my tension, but I still wondered how Travis felt about their *friendship*. I had trouble being friends with females without someone's feelings and heart getting involved.

"Enough about me," she said suddenly, catching me off guard. "Tell me something about you."

"What do you want to know?" I asked, eyeing her curiously.

"Anything."

I racked my brain for something, anything I could tell her of the same caliber to what she shared with me. "When I was fifteen, my mother said she was going to the store for milk and would be right back. I never saw her again..."

I had never told anyone that story. Not even Madalynne. Sharing the story with Jacqueline felt right. Especially with how much she had been through in her life.

"I'm sorry..." she replied almost instantly, an empathetic look taking over her face.

"For the first few years I blamed myself for her disappearance. Wondered if there was something I could have done. I had no idea if she left our family by choice or if something terrible happened to her." Remembering that dark time had tears stinging the back of my eyes. I quickly looked out my window, determined to blink them back.

Jacqueline remained quiet, almost willing me to continue telling my story.

"It affected my brother worse. He was only nine at the time. He searched for her for close to ten years before my father convinced him she was never coming back. My father has since remarried…but not knowing what really happened to her almost destroyed us all in different ways."

Jacqueline was the one squeezing my hand then. Letting me know she was there for me. "Thank you."

"For what?"

"For sharing something so personal with me. I know how difficult it must have been to tell me that." She smiled lightly at me.

I brought her hand up to my lips and kissed it gently then.

"We're here," she whispered as we pulled up to the enormous mountain where we would be spending the day in the snow.

It was packed and buzzing as we exited her car and headed towards the entrance.

*   *   *

"Fuck snowboarding, fuck you, and fuck this!" Jacqueline hissed at me, her face red from the wind. I couldn't help but laugh. It had to be the tenth time she had fallen on her butt. I never said snowboarding was going to be a piece of cake—and I had taught handfuls of friends the sport...but I had underestimated her.

She was spicy, bullheaded, and impatient. "Maybe this wasn't such a good idea...but I never pictured you a quitter."

I saw rage cross her eyes under her goggles. "Quitting?" She basically screamed back at me. "I've fallen on my ass more times than I can count because of you! Not to mention I can't even feel my fingers or toes—and it's all your fault."

I chuckled again. "So, you don't enjoy snowboarding, but at least you got to experience it, right? Let's focus on the positives here."

"Stop laughing at me!" She shoved me angrily before stomping off in the opposite direction, away from her board, leaving it beside me.

"Jacqueline! I can't carry both boards!" I yelled to her turned back.

"This was your idea genius, figure it out!" I heard her yell back over her shoulder.

I shook my head. Bipolar didn't suit her. And as much as I was beginning to fall for her, her mood swings were a huge turn-off for me. What I had anticipated to be a fun day had turned into a cold, irritating day. I wanted nothing more than to be bundled up inside my hotel room, away from her whiny voice.

After managing to carry both boards, I turned in all my gear and found Jacqueline standing outside of her car smoking a cigarette. "I didn't know you smoked," I said as I approached slowly.

"I don't." She answered simply, taking another drag off the cancer stick.

"Then why are you now?" I asked, taking it out of her lips, and throwing it into the snow. Smoking cigarettes was a huge turn-off to me. That smell could seep into anything—hair, skin, clothes, her mouth.

"What the hell?" She pushed me again roughly.

"You can stop being a bitch now." I was losing my patience with her, one word at a time. "You know very well I had not anticipated you having such a terrible time at the mountain. I was only trying to enjoy our time together."

She slapped me then, it was so loud, I was sure it was the smack heard around the world. I rubbed my face, gingerly. "I think I've had just about enough of your bipolar ways for one day." I didn't bother giving her another glance as I climbed in the car.

"Oh no you don't!" She screamed as she raced to my door, which I swiftly locked. She was banging on it. "Get out of my car!"

She was causing a scene and I watched as bystanders began to take interest into our little fight. After she became aware of the fact, she hastily climbed into the driver's seat.

"Get the fuck out of my car!" She was still screaming at me, but now we were in close proximity.

"Or what? You've already mastered slapping, pushing, punching...what else could you possibly do to me?" I knew my words had made an impact when I saw her look away quickly.

She started the car then, and we drove the entire way back in silence. I was surprised when I heard her sniffle. I looked over at her and realized she was crying. Even though she was the one in the wrong, my exterior suddenly softened at the sight of her crying. I didn't say anything, just rubbed her hand softly which was resting on the gear shift.

When she pulled up to my hotel, I reached for the handle when she stopped me by throwing out her arm in front of me. "I'm fucked up…I know that. I'm sorry for being a bitch."

"It's okay," I said out of habit.

"No it's not. You didn't deserve any of that back there. I really appreciate you trying to help me experience life more." Tears were falling down her cheeks now and she was having trouble speaking without awkward pauses.

"To be fair, you did warn me…"

"It's no excuse. I am going to begin taking my medicine again." She wiped away her tears with the back of her sleeve.

"Why did you stop taking them?" I asked, curiously.

"They turn me into a zombie; devoid of any sort of feeling. They make me feel empty."

"But would you rather be stable or unstable?" I asked the necessary question.

She shrugged. "It doesn't really matter anymore. I obviously can't be trusted off them. Plus Travis has been trying to convince me to get back on them for years."

The thought that her best friend had attempted to help her for years and she tuned it out—only to listen to me, a stranger, intrigued me.

"Do you want to come in?" I found myself asking.

"I think I've done enough damage for one night," she said softly, staring out her side window.

"Yeah, but I forgive you and I want to spend more time getting to know you." I didn't know why I was letting her off the hook so easily, but knowing somewhat of her troubled past, I couldn't fathom not going easy on her.

"You're wasting your time," she replied.

I grabbed her chin then, tilting it towards me. "You're not a waste of time to me. You're not a lost cause. I'm telling you I forgive you and want to spend more time with you. Now are you coming in or not?"

I didn't have to ask again…she was out of the car quicker than I could have ever imagined. I guess I got my answer.

Thirteen – Don't Look Back

Jacqueline

My breathing intensified, coming out in short stints. His fingers were cupping my face in the most delicate way. Our lips had been tangled up in one another's since he invited me up and we hadn't even taken a break.

We had been rolling back and forth on the queen bed, my legs entangled with his.

So far Lee had been the upmost gentleman, only kissing me passionately and deeply. He had stayed well behaved and his hands had remained in my hair or on my face, but I could tell he was getting worked up by each and every nibble on his lip, tug on his hair.

He was pressing into me with each and every kiss as if trying to discover new territory.

He climbed on top of me then, his hand sliding slowly down my arm, reaching for my shirt. He hadn't missed a beat, still kissing me deeply.

His hands were reaching for the bottom of my sweater, sliding softly across my hip, making me shiver.

I hadn't intended for it to go this far. In fact, I was pretty sure I wanted to wait a bit longer before going all the way, but while my mind was saying no, my body was saying the opposite. I found myself allowing Lee to remove my sweater revealing my black lacy bra.

He wasted no time kissing my shoulder gingerly before removing my bra straps, letting my breasts fall out naturally.

I saw the hunger in Lee's eyes, the intensity— it was the same as the first night, the one in my car—but more so.

Lee took one of my breasts in his mouth and sucked and tugged gently on the nipple with his teeth, making me moan out with pleasure.

He was trailing my neck then with his tongue making me stir and shake against his touch. I was grinding against him.

He twirled me around so I was on top and I quickly lowered my lips to his, sucking gently on his bottom lip. I took note as he pressed roughly into me. His erect penis was hard to ignore.

Stop.

My mind was trying to convince me, knowing he wasn't ready to experience all of me yet.

My loud moans kept me in place, making me forget why I wasn't going to allow this to happen.

It wasn't even until he reached for my belt that the sense finally got knocked into me.

"I can't do this…" I trailed off breathlessly.

"What?" Lee asked, exasperated.

"You heard me. I can't do this. I'm not ready."

Lee looked at me incredulously, then back to the crotch of his pants. I had undoubtedly left him with blue balls.

"You've got to be kidding me…" Lee grumbled upset.

"I'll let myself out." And that's exactly what I did after gathering my clothes, I made a swift exit without another glance.

*   *   *

Our time together was coming to its end and as diligent as I had been, I wasn't sure I could hold him off this time, so I dressed in my sexiest stockings along with my lacy bra and matching panties. As long as he didn't see my legs, it was fine.

We were at my house, on my couch aggressively making out.

Lee had come over hours earlier and we had watched Anchorman before jumping each other. He was lying on top of me, thrusting into me as he pressed his lips against mine.

Our tongues had aggressively wrestled until he softly took my bottom lip between his teeth and sucked on it lightly, causing me to moan out with pleasure.

I didn't wait for Lee to take the lead then. I quickly pulled his sweatshirt off, surprising him. He was smiling naughtily back at me. He kissed me quickly then.

I ran my hands over his wife beater and his dark chest. Gripping my fingernails into his shoulder anytime he thrust against me.

He lifted my long sleeve shirt along with my tank right off in one fell swoop. Then laid me back down and pressed his lips gently along my stomach and then along my collarbone, raising goose bumps all over my body.

He picked me up, lifting me effortlessly into the air and carried me to my bedroom. He went to reach for the light, when I stopped him. "Don't."

He didn't seem to pay it any mind. Just carried me to the middle of the room and then laid me gently on the bed.

He climbed on top of me in the darkness and we continued to make out passionately.

I felt his hands at the button of my jeans, but didn't stop him his time—my hands were following his instruction.

I could feel the soft fabric of his boxer briefs as well as the hardness and stiffness of his dick.

I gently grazed the erect tip with my hand, enough to drive him crazy.

My pants were off without another blink.

His fingers were exploring every inch of me and just when I thought I couldn't take anymore he was kissing the inside of my thighs—making every inch of me tremble with pleasure.

And then I felt it—intense gratification, my body jerking violently from it.

The heat only increased from there as I felt him enter me, a burning, intense, rough pleasure unlike any other.

He was rubbing his hands up and down my stockings unaware they hid my scars. He was thrusting deeper and I was pulling him in closer, wrapping my legs around his body, only bringing us tighter.

I couldn't see his expression, but I could feel him, inside me. Our breathing had become a unit. I had never felt closer to anyone in my life.

When I heard him moan "Jacqueline," my name, I quickly sucked on the bottom of his ear, while digging my fingernails gently into his back, his shoulders. I loved the way he shuddered from it and then I felt him come. He was breathing heavily and deeply and I realized something in that moment—I had never felt more passion in my entire life.

Lee

As great as the sex was, her clinger status and obvious secrets were a little alarming.

I had been home in Hawaii for a week and Jacqueline had managed to call me three times and text me nine. All were met with silence. When someone liked me, this quick, this fast— I ran the other way every time as if on cue. Jacqueline was no different.

I wanted to remain friends—I didn't want to push her away entirely but she was coming on just a bit too strong for my taste.

I knew how fragile she was though. I knew if I gave her an inch, she'd steal a mile. I knew we both weren't ready for a full blown committed relationship; we both had issues that needed to be addressed.

So I cut off all communication. It was the only way; a clean break. I deleted and blocked her on my messenger services along with Facebook, then blacklisted her number so I couldn't receive calls or texts from her. It was low of me, I know, but I had to do it.

And then I went straight into my guilt-driven destruction mode. Booze—girls—what I was best at.

It didn't mean that I didn't come home and stare at my computer screen for hours contemplating apologizing. Wondering how she was taking my disappearance. I felt like the biggest ass on the face of the planet. But I never broke. My stone, cold façade held up along with my ice cold heart.

I had thrown myself so entirely back into work, my entire body was sore. I was barely walking normal from the ass kicking I had given myself in the gym when one of my regular clients Kim, eyed me up and down like I was a piece of meat.

We had had our history, Kim and me. It mainly consisted of drunken hook-ups only one of us could remember clearly the next morning and one unforgettable pregnancy scare. I hadn't ventured back since it scared me shitless, but I couldn't deny how sexy it was that she never broke a sweat once in my kick-butt work out. It was a rarity almost never seen.

Her long brown hair cascaded over her shoulders and her side swept bangs were enough to make any guy tongue-tied.

Her chocolate eyes stared into mine deeply. "Lee," she murmured.

"Kim," I followed her lead.

"So you never finished telling me about Montana." She wiped the back of her neck with a towel.

"There's not much to tell. It was cold and miserable."

"Well that's unfortunate," she replied, biting her bottom lip playfully, still eye-fucking me.

I shrugged. "No biggie." I wiped the sweat beads off my face and picked up my gym bag.

"Got any plans tonight?" Kim asked, in tow with me.

I glanced down at her. "Yeah, I have a date with my pillow." It wasn't entirely a lie, I hadn't been sleeping all that well the past week.

She smiled shyly back at me. "Well if you find yourself bored, I'm having a few people over to my place. It'd be fun to hang out like old times."

I smiled back at her with my most charming smile, one that could deceive anyone with a heart. "I'll definitely keep that in mind. You did a great job today Kim, I'm really impressed."

She blushed then, looking away embarrassed. "I have a really great trainer."

I smiled once more, then exited the building towards my car. I needed no reassurance. I knew I was the world's best trainer.

I turned on my car and the first song that came on hit me like a ton of bricks. It was *Royals* by Lorde, it was all the craze and very much overplayed, but it only made me think of one thing…or should I say one person, Jacqueline.

She had made me listen to the Lorde cd on repeat my entire trip—but secretly I loved every second of it. I came to love the haunting voice in the tracks and knew almost all the words to the cd by the time she dropped me off at the airport the last day.

Those were the last lyrics I heard as I climbed out of her car that chilly December morning. Those were the words that convinced me we could never work. They were what caused me to push her away.

I gave her a long hug and brushed my lips against hers stiffly before turning my back and walking away—leaving her behind.

Fourteen – Radio Silence

Jacqueline

I had been duped.

Yep, you heard me right. I, Jacqueline Blunt had opened my heart for only the second time in my life only to have it crushed.

The worst part about it was not knowing why he never returned my texts—my phone calls.

After all of the radio silence I got from Lee, I decided not to dwell on it any more. Why was I wasting my time and energy on someone who wouldn't do the same for me?

It was the most rational I had been in years. It felt like my medicine was actually working this time. It surprised me.

Lee had left for Hawaii almost three weeks ago and I had spent practically every day with Travis. I began to see him through different eyes. Anyone who could handle that much of me was special. Travis never ran; I never scared him away. In fact, I had never felt closer to him in my entire life.

The new feelings were overwhelming and unexpected. And the reappearance of butterflies in my stomach was enough to make anyone nauseous.

Travis knew me. He knew almost all of me—more than anyone else—and it didn't scare him away. I found myself daydreaming of his dashing smile and kind eyes. He was handsome, undoubtedly.

Am I really entertaining this idea?

Yes, yes…in fact, for the first time in my entire life I could picture my best friend in the romantic sense. He never pursued me—pressured me, but I could feel us growing closer with each passing night.

Last night we had been watching a movie and fell asleep…together. I awoke to his arms wrapped around me tightly and he had this smirk plastered across his face; all the while dead asleep. I liked the feeling of being in his arms…it felt safe.

He didn't know it, but I kissed him while he was sleeping. I couldn't help it…he just looked so peaceful. It was only a peck—and light as a feather—but I couldn't deny that things had changed.

"Are you okay?" Travis asked me from the other side of the couch. He had come over an hour earlier for our usual Walking Dead night, but I was having trouble acting normal after the epiphany I had had.

I swallowed loudly, attempting to come up with the best answer—the one that would get him off my back.

"Yeah, I'm fine," I replied in a small voice.

"Well, are you cold?"

I shook my head no, silently.

"Then why are you shaking like that?"

I looked down at my body quickly then. He was right—I was shaking something fierce. Travis was making me nervous...when had that *ever* happened?

My behavior was surprising the both of us. I could feel him inching closer—the hammering of my heart against my chest.

"Why are you acting so strange?" He nudged me playfully with his shoulder.

I looked down and away, afraid if he saw my eyes, he would realize what I had...I had been blind for far too long.

I wince as I hear my stomach grumble loudly.

"Whoa, was that you?" Travis laughs, unable to stop himself.

I shove him gently before opening my locker to grab my English textbook out.

"When is the last time you ate?" Travis asks, no apparent concern for overstepping.

"I had lunch," I whisper, my stomach taking on a starring role with its loudness. I blush, embarrassed.

"We haven't even had lunch yet," Travis chuckles softly before it hit him. "Wait...you're talking about lunch yesterday?"

I can't even look him in the eye.

"What is going on now?" Travis eyes me down sympathetically.

"LaToya is just being a bitch," I answer, wishing it was as simple as that.

"What did you do?" Travis asks, his eyebrows raising animatedly.

I hold my hands up in the air, in surrender. "I didn't do anything—I swear."

Travis cracks a smile. "Come on, we're going to be late for class." He tugs on my arm, leading the way.

*   *   *

My stomach is eating itself, burning me from the inside. A pain I am becoming far too familiar with…

Normally I would count down the minutes until I got to eat, but today is different…Janice and LaToya jumped me before school and stole the small bit of lunch money I had.

So much for quieting the monster in my stomach down.

Even though being in the cafeteria is going to be the worst kind of torture—it is something I will have to learn to endure because Travis is not going to change his routine for me.

I plop myself down next to Travis just as the bell signaling lunch silences.

He stares at me and my empty hands. "No lunch today?"

115

I shrug, doing my best not to let him pity me. I can take care of myself. "Not hungry," I lie as my stomach growls louder than I've ever heard before.

Travis opens his brown bag, the one his mother has been packing him since kindergarten and then looks back at me.

"Turkey or ham?"

"Huh?" I ask, clueless, watching him reach into the paper bag and pull out two sandwiches.

My eyes are fixated on the sandwich in his left hand. I can basically feel my mouth salivating. I don't say a word, just grab the turkey sandwich out of his hands. I'm pretty sure I inhale the entire thing in one bite. Nothing has ever tasted as heavenly.

Over the rest of the year, he continues to bring a lunch for the both of us. I don't know what I did to deserve him…but he is the reason I wake up in the morning from my shitty life and vow to be a better person. He is the most incredible best friend a girl could ever ask for.

Fifteen – Total Blackout

Lee

"Is that all you've got?" I egged Austyn on. She was in Hawaii visiting for a few days and I hadn't let her rest for a second. She was one of the only people in the world who could keep up with me—I chucked it up to all of our play time as children.

Austyn gave me a death glare, sending me into a round of chuckles to which were met with harder punches, faster kicks.

I held the bag tightly as she let out her rage for me out on it, before she finally fell to the floor, breathing deeply.

"Much better." I crouched beside her.

"Thanks douche," she laughed then grabbed for her towel and wiped her face and neck off.

"I wish more of my clients were like you." I took a swig off of my water bottle.

"What? Put up with your shit?" She stuck her tongue out at me playfully.

"No, just up for the challenge."

"What happened with Jacqueline?" She went there. As much as Austyn knew I hated talking about my relationships, she knew I couldn't lie to her.

"It just didn't work out," I answered simply, standing up, hoping she would drop it, but she didn't take the hint.

"Was she ugly?" She asked; Jacqueline's angelic face popped into my head then.

"No."

"Is she a bitch?" Austyn pressed, jumping to her feet.

I sighed loudly, taking a few steps toward the doors. "Kind of, look it's complicated—will you drop it?"

"Why do you always do this?" Austyn asked then, walking towards me.

"Do what?" I asked, clueless.

"Push away the people who care about you most?" She had hit the nail on the head.

"I don't know what you're talking about," I continued with my denial.

"You don't even have to tell me...I can read it all over your face. She came on too strong and it scared you off." Austyn's assessment of me was spot on, unfortunately.

"It's so much more than that Austyn..." I trailed off as I began walking towards the locker rooms.

"Oh yeah? What scared Lee Bennett off—tell me," she challenged me.

I lowered my voice as we weren't alone and closed the distance between us. "Listen, she's unstable—she is bipolar—and I'm positive that's not her only secret.

"Oh boo-hoo, when has Lee Bennett ever shied away from a challenge? I think a little crazy is exactly what you need."

Her response had me all sorts of confused. My mind was at an all-time tug-of-war in the shower, on the drive home from the gym, and now back in the solace of my own house.

Austyn skipped the shower at the gym and had opted to wait until we returned to my house. When I heard the water of the shower ricocheting off the glass, I hopped on my computer.

It didn't take me long to realize that Jacqueline was online. I had unblocked her a few days ago out of curiosity and had planned to re-block her—it just hadn't happened yet.

I opened a conversation to type to her multiple times, only to close it out in the end, nothing in the box.

Did I really want to open the gates of hell? Jacqueline was a handful—I was learning this firsthand. Was I really ready for all that...crazy?

The answer was no when I heard the bathroom door begin to creak open and I closed out of the messenger service entirely.

Jacqueline

I had never planned it. Oddly enough it always seemed to be a reckless last minute decision that landed me in these situations.

I was doing the dishes when I heard the phone ring. After turning the faucet off and drying my hands I answered on the fourth ring.

It was a recording. *This is a collect call from an inmate inside the Montana Department of Corrections. To accept this call press one.*

My heart was in my throat; my eyes darting around the room rapidly. There was only one inmate I knew—my mother. Someone I hadn't heard from since I was thirteen.

One push and I would be reunited with my mother of the year…curiosity got the best of me as I accepted the call.

"Jacquie? Jacquie? Are you there?" It was surprising to me that after five years I could recognize her hoarse voice.

"It's Jacqueline," I answered after a few minutes of silence.

"Jacqueline, right, listen up, I missed you baby."

I wanted to jump through the phone and strangle her. If it wasn't for my medicine calming me down and the obvious obstacles between us, I might have actually gone postal.

121

"How are you? Are you good?" Her questions broke into my thoughts.

The fact that she was being friendly and acting as if nothing ever happened was driving me nuts.

"I'm fine, no thanks to you." My words came out like a tight whip.

"Look, I understand that you're angry with me. But I want to make it up to you." I couldn't believe what I was hearing.

"Make it up to me? Not possible," I hissed, angrily.

"I was calling to invite you to the DOC so we could talk." Her voice never wavered, I had to give it to her.

"And what could we possibly have to talk about?" I snapped.

"Anything—everything."

I slammed the phone closed without another word. She was asking too much. She knew exactly what she put me through as a child and although she knew nothing of my life in foster care, I wanted to avoid that conversation altogether if possible.

I couldn't see straight—couldn't think straight—just went into autopilot, locking myself into the bathroom and reaching for my blade.

That was the last thing I remembered. Then suddenly there were loud bangs and I could faintly hear someone yelling my name.

"Jacqueline, open this door now."

Boom.

Travis?

My eyes were fluttering open and closed. I was fighting my weakness with everything I had in me.

The last thing I caught was the bathroom door roughly being kicked in and then the darkness took me over.

Sixteen – Forbidden Feelings

Lee

"Pour me another," I droned to my usual bartender at my usual hole in the wall.

"Another one of those nights?" She asked, her eyebrows raising.

"Please Ashli, I'm not in the mood," I yawned, acting as bored as possible.

"Fine, but don't expect me to listen to any more to your useless ramblings." She slammed my drink down next to me then stomped away, her butt firm as ever.

Normally I would be willing to eat M&M's off that ass. But as of late, I was having trouble even arousing myself.

There was something missing in my life.

Passion.

I had been fooling myself thinking that I could ever find anyone comparable to Taylor—she was truly one of a kind.

I didn't want anyone like Madalynne because I was afraid of my heart being risked again.

And then as unstable and reckless as she was—there was Jacqueline. I swear that woman was driving me nuts.

Part of it was how I couldn't get her out of my mind. Even after blocking her—I still awoke from dreams and nightmares alike where she had a starring role.

It had been months since we had last spoken and I had been on countless dates with other women, but all paled in comparison to her—how was that?

I'll tell you what it was—it was her spiciness—she always kept me guessing.

I was tired of going through the same repetitive days, routines, even schedules. It was always the same. I was losing my zest for life—for love. I needed something to shake up the ordinary.

My heart began to race out of control; my palms instantly sweaty. My breathing became stiff and stilted.

If someone would have told me a month ago that I would be doing this—I would have laughed in their face.

Yet, there I was, still as a board, my phone in my hand—and a familiar number and name highlighted.

I squeezed my eyes closed tightly and held my breath as I pressed call…

Jacqueline

"Give it back!" I pouted sprawled across Travis' lap, reaching for the remote.

"Come and get it," he taunted playfully, a mischievous grin taking over his face.

"Maybe I will!" I shot back as I pounced even harder onto him.

We had been near inseparable since the *incident*. We had avoided the conversation altogether—something we had become all too familiar with, but Travis had been a constant in my everyday life since he found me, and we were growing understandably close. It didn't help that I felt forever indebted to him for taking care of me that day—for being my savior.

I heard snapping in front of my face.

"What the hell?" I asked, coming back to reality.

"Where did you just go then?" Travis asked, referring to my space out.

"Nowhere." I shrugged.

"Right." I watched as he rolled his eyes then instantly shifted the power by pouncing on me. His big strong body was on top of mine on the couch and if that wasn't enough, he had taken to tickling me.

I was laughing so hard at one point that I lost my breath. I was grasping at my sore sides, attempting to massage out the laugh pains I was getting—when I saw the expression change on Travis' face.

I knew then that it was going to happen—our first kiss.

I was swallowing repeatedly, trying to get past my cottonmouth. I was about to kiss my best friend…and I didn't deserve him.

I puckered my lips as his inched closer, closing my eyes.

This was it. In a few seconds I would be kissing Travis. The mystery would be over. Of course I had wondered about this moment…he was a handsome devil.

When I didn't instantly feel his lips on mine, I slowly peeked out of one of my eyes only to catch Travis staring down at the coffee table, my cell phone vibrating wildly.

My mind was racing.

Should I answer it?

It seemed like such a buzzkill. It had ruined our near perfect moment, but with Travis' eyes burning holes into me, I swallowed then maneuvered myself out from under him before I went to reach for it.

I glanced at the illuminated screen before pressing the button to answer.

There was no way.

The name staring back on the screen of my phone along with his irritatingly beautiful smile had my heart racing a mile a minute.

Lee was calling me.

Lee was calling me and Travis was sitting next to me; we had just been about to kiss. It was a catch-22.

If I answered, I could almost picture the curiosity and sadness in his eyes. If I passed it up, I would play the what-if game until eternity. See what I said? A catch-22.

"Are you going to answer that?" Travis tried to catch a glimpse of the screen of my phone, obviously trying to solve the riddle of who my mystery caller was.

I pulled the phone closer to me, took a deep, silent breath, and then clicked the green button to pick it up.

"Hello?" I answered, breathlessly, my heart thumping loudly.

"Hello?" I asked again, only to be met with silence.

Click.

Son of a bitch.

Seventeen – Left For Dead

Lee

"Hey man! Wait up!" I heard my friend and client shout from behind my back.

"Oh, sorry dude." I slowed my pace so Dan could catch up.

He was huffing and puffing like I had never seen him do before. "Are you okay? Do you want some of my water?"

Had I really been going that fast? The idea was absurd—it was normal for me to finish the mile in four minutes—so any quicker than that and Dan probably thought I was on crack.

He was still catching his breath when I handed him my water bottle. "I'm sorry man, I had no idea I was running that fast." Honestly, it all felt like a bit of a blur to me.

"Like a bat out of hell?" Dan finally choked out.

I chuckled. "I said I'm sorry okay?"

He finally cracked a smile. "So, what has been up with you lately? You've been hard to track down."

I shrugged my shoulders as I wiped the back of my hand across my drenched forehead.

"Do you ever think about settling down?" I asked as he handed my water bottle back to me.

"Like with one woman?" Dan asked for clarification as I took a swig of my water.

I nodded my head, remaining silent.

"Oh God no! Not when there is so much grade A pussy in the world! I'm not well versed yet in all the different types...Vietnamese, Australian, Belgian...I'll probably entertain the idea in ten years."

"Dan, you're thirty," I pointed out.

"And your point?" He looked at me like I had sprouted a second head. "Listen Lee, I admire you for your ambition to go down such a road—but I'm not one for self-destruction."

"Ambition?" I looked into his eyes—angry he had made such an assumption. "You don't think I can do it, do you?"

132

"What? Stop fucking the entire female race? No, I don't think you can do it. We're creatures of habit, you and me. It's in our nature. We're cut from the same cloth. Sue me."

I pushed him roughly away from me. "I can and I will—and you can find a new trainer from now on."

I began to walk away from Dan when I heard his deep voice behind me. "Oh, you'll be back. You always come back. Nothing compares to freedom."

I turned around so we were now facing each other. "See, that's where you're wrong—if forced to make a choice, I'd choose love every time…guess we're not cut from the same cloth after all." And with that I turned my back to the douchebag I used to call my friend.

A weight felt like it had been lifted off of my heart. I knew then what I had to do…

* * *

A few hours later I was seated at my kitchen table with a number two pencil and a stack of blank sheets of paper.

At first I sat there, just staring at the blank pages, waiting for something to happen...and then suddenly words were flowing freely through my fingers and to the paper.

Jacqueline,

It's been over a month since we last talked. I know I don't deserve a second of your time, but suppose you're still reading this—then I would say you terrify me.

Jacqueline

Since I was a little girl and I began self-harming I always hoped and dreamt and wished for someone who would love me for me and take me away from the pain...someone who would help me fight my addiction; someone who could help me curb it; someone I would love more than *it*.

At first, I thought that someone was going to be Parker—but that was short lived.

And then there was the minor stint I like to call Lee, or rather the mistake...and then, after knowing him my entire life and never thinking of him that way, Travis, but something wasn't right; something felt off.

The burning desire to bring the blade to my flesh had intensified and was overwhelming.

Why wasn't my fairy tale working out?

Earlier, somehow, Travis and I had fallen asleep together on my bed—completely innocent. I had woken up around three a.m., I knew because my bedside clock was illuminated as I slipped out.

I hadn't planned on ending up here…especially with Travis in my bed, but after perusing the fridge for five long minutes I couldn't stand it anymore, and I ended up back in the same spot and position I had hungered for with every inch of my being.

Because of my last big *incident,* I didn't have the courtesy of a bathroom door yet—Travis had planned on replacing it, just got wrapped up with, well…me.

So as to draw as little attention as possible, I was doing it in the dark—basically blind.

As my skin ripped open, I tilted my head back, taking a deep breath—this was my release…*this* was what I lived for.

I didn't hear him through my euphoria—but the bright light assaulting the corners of my eyelids told me I had been caught.

Not two seconds later and I felt the blade being ripped out of my hand and then just as my eyes flew open I was met with a rough slap across the face.

I grabbed at my sore cheek, my eyes the size of tennis balls. I couldn't believe Travis had just hit me.

"It's the only way I knew I could get you to listen," Travis's voice came out in stilted breaths. "I'm tired of fighting for you when you won't even fight for yourself."

I was still rubbing my cheek but not so much to ease the pain—more so as a calming effect, because I was pretty sure Travis was done with me.

And then he said the words that would crush me.

"I can't do this anymore."

"No!" I shrieked, falling instantly at his feet— the thought of losing Travis was tearing me apart. "Don't leave me, I can't do this without you!"

Travis remained still, my arms tightly wrapped around his right leg; holding on for dear life.

"Get up J," Travis boomed from above my head.

I remained crouched on the ground, still sobbing when Travis's voice came through again.

"Stand up Jacqueline."

He didn't have to say it a third time; my legs needed no further instruction. I was standing staring up into Travis's sad brown eyes and dejected face.

Yeah fucker—you did this.

"Get help J, before it's too late." And then he reached his hand up to softly rub the spot he had hit earlier.

Before I even knew what was happening he leaned in. His lips brushed up against mine with a bit of urgency and sadness. I was trying to pull him in, closer—when he suddenly ripped away from me.

"Get that cleaned up before you bleed out." He was pointing to my open gash.

I glanced at it, my cheeks burning up. He was right, there were drips of blood all over the floor.

"Goodbye Jacqueline." And then he was gone—and my legs crumpled underneath me. All that was left was my limp body on the floor of the bathroom—bawling my eyes out.

How will I ever get through this without him?

Eighteen – Small Steps for Mankind

Lee

Jacqueline,

It's been over a month since we last talked. I know I don't deserve a second of your time, but suppose you're still reading this—then I would say you <u>terrify</u> me.

I have only ever loved two people. Two polar opposites. Taylor and Madalynne. Taylor was my high school sweetheart, I always imagined my happy ending with her, and then she was violently ripped away from this world. They said she died on impact; that she hadn't felt an ounce of pain. I wanted to believe that more than anything.

The semi-truck driver had fallen asleep at the wheel— a freak accident they called it. He made it out scotch free, nothing more than a few minor scratches and bruises. Can you imagine knowing you are solely responsible for ending someone's life? He definitely got what he deserved, a life full of memories and regret that will eventually eat him alive.

After Taylor, I couldn't fathom ever caring for another to that extent again, so I became another version of myself—a darker version; one fond of alcohol and one night stands—someone who was content without getting feelings involved. I became the ultimate player and I reveled in it. Knowing I could have any girl I wanted? It was a very powerful feeling...

And then Maddy entered my life and showed me what I had been missing for all those years. She reminded me the love that I had in me to give to another person, but as quickly as she came, she went, and chose someone else over me...Parker. But you know this story already.

What you didn't know was how difficult it was for me to let my guard down and let Maddy in—it terrified me. After her, my walls went up double time. I became bitter and resentful. I became a person I'm not proud of.

Alcohol became the solution to all my problems—numbing the pain, but the drinking and bad decisions only pushed those around me away.

What you don't know, what I haven't told anyone, is that I want to be a good person. I want to be monogamous. I want those terrifying, gut-wrenching feelings again even though it scares the shit out of me. I can't live my life afraid anymore.

Jacqueline, you are the first person since Maddy who gave me a run for my money—who didn't put up with my shit; who challenged me.

I felt passion and emotion when we had sex. It felt right...something I kept deep inside myself until now. It was easier to run then, so I did—like the coward I was.

But I am back and I am standing before you begging your forgiveness and for another chance. I know I don't deserve it, after all the shit I've pulled, but I hope you decide to put all your inhibitions aside and trust me.

I know you're hiding something from me and while I can speculate forever, the truth is I just want you to trust me enough to tell me what it is.

I could tell you were broken from a mile away...but it was beautiful. You were beautiful.

I want you to know that while you frustrate me to no end, you turn me on more than anyone I've ever met in my entire life. It's something about your sauciness and comebacks. Everything is so passionate with you—I almost feel like we balance each other out. You're fire and I'm ice.

We could either be the best or the worst person for one another, but I'm willing to take a leap of faith if you are.

No more secrets. No more lies. I want you…

What I'm trying to say is, let's scare the shit out of each other.

Always,
Lee

Jacqueline

It had been a week since Travis had left me…behind. I hadn't moved an inch from my bed in that time other than to eat and drink very little and use the restroom. My eyes were swollen from tears. My phone had been ringing off the hook with his mother's number—my boss, but I couldn't bear to speak to anyone. I just wanted it all to end. I just wanted to silence the pain.

I had contemplated three extremely serious ways of ending it all, and the only thing that had halted my plan was Travis's nagging words in my ear. I wanted to prove him wrong. I wanted to show him that yes, I was broken, but worthy of being fixed.

So what if he had lost faith in me? I was used to being let down my entire life…I needed to start sticking up for myself at some point. So I wiped my tears away, pushed away the covers, and took my first steps toward my new future.

I only made it to the mailbox, but hey, I was willing to celebrate the small victories if need be.

I pulled the mound of mail out of it and stuffed it all under my arm, running back across the parking lot to my apartment.

I threw the stack on the table and kicked off my shoes. It all looked so overwhelming, something that would normally have me spinning out of control—but there, amongst the ads, the bills, the postcards was a bright red envelope—if that didn't demand attention, I wasn't sure what would.

I hurriedly pulled it from the pile, staring intently at the address label. *It can't be...*

I ripped it open without another thought; my heart pounding wildly.

It was a letter from Lee.

Nineteen – A Growing Fascination

Lee

Hawaii was warm and pleasant, sunny and beautiful. I had awoken with the sun and enjoyed a good two hours of killer waves.

Once I made it home, I quickly stripped off my wetsuit and hopped into the shower letting the hot water trickle down my back—my head deep in thought.

I hadn't let myself go there—to think about her because I half expected never to hear from her again—but it didn't mean I wondered any less what she thought after reading my epic handwritten letter.

I was hoping it would help her understand where I had been coming from; help her understand me. I wanted to explain why I had been such an asshole and why I couldn't move past my own issues to jump head first in with her. For all I knew, I had lost my chance.

I ran my hand over my short, wet hair, sighing softly. I had really put myself out there; the first time since the Madalynne scandal. The thought of caring for anyone as much as I had for Taylor or Madalynne with the possibility of losing them was an immobilizing feeling.

Damn it Jacqueline.

She could be my destruction; my demise. I told her I was basically willing to relinquish all power, a ballsy move for someone like myself.

After drying off and getting dressed, I picked up my cell pressing speed dial number one. A familiar high pitched voice answered on the fourth ring.

"I'm going to tell you this—but I'm only going to tell you once; I'm ready to stop being afraid."

I heard a long spout of air being released on the other end after my confession. "You have no idea how long I have been waiting for you to say that."

"I want to be a good person Austyn, I'm tired of hurting innocent people—I'm tired of running from my problems." My answer was surprising, yet sincere.

"What happened to you?" Austyn asked, dumbfounded; surprised I was willing to relinquish my player ways for one girl.

"She changed me Austyn. I don't know what it is, but she drives me crazy in the best and worst possible ways. She challenges me—doesn't put up with my shit. She *needs* me."

"Whoa, remember you want to live your life for *you*. Not for some other person."

I nodded before realizing she couldn't see me. "I am doing this for myself Austyn—I want her in my life...and as much as she needs me, I think I need her."

"Please tell me we are talking about a spunky blond," Austyn gushed.

"Of course we are, who else would we be talking about?" I chuckled into my receiver.

"With you—virtually anyone! God Lee, I am so proud of you. You are growing up." Austyn's voice was soft and genuine.

"Thanks cuz," I said before exchanging goodbyes. Without missing a beat, I anxiously raced outside to check my mailbox. It had been close to three weeks since I had sent my letter—but I had been watching my mail closely; waiting, hoping for anything.

As I pulled the pile that had been squished into my tiny assigned box, I saw it. It appeared to be a card. I ripped it open without bothering to see if it was even from *her*.

The card was blank on the inside, except for one sentence scribbled neatly on the inside:

Lilies are my favorite type of flower.

I cracked a smile instantly, she was letting me in; it was the olive branch I had been wishing for.

Before I had completely comprehended what my body was doing, I was texting Jacqueline...I couldn't help myself. *Lilies eh? No love for roses? They're a classic.*

Even though I was a little upset she hadn't addressed any part of my letter, I was thankful she was giving me an in of any kind—large or small.

Following that day I received about a letter a week—our communication growing daily.

Jacqueline

His letter was…something else. There was no way I could ignore him after I read it and really gave it the attention it deserved…after I digested all of his confessions.

The texts and phone calls followed shortly after; the intrigue growing more and more with each and every one.

We had such a strange history and story—I wanted to go slow this time. Really get to know one another before jumping straight back into bed.

I wasn't prepared when he brought up my secret while on the phone late one night. He asked a direct question pertaining to my legs. It really startled me. How sloppy had I been when he had visited?

There was no way he would want to give us a shot if he knew how invested I still was with my addiction.

"Why do you do it Jac? Is it because you've become accustomed to it? Is it because you crave it? Or is it because you don't feel good enough about yourself?"
I couldn't form a proper answer.

"What can I do to help? What needs to happen to change your focus?"

I swallowed loudly, this was really happening. I was discussing my dark addiction with Lee, and even though my heart was racing beyond control, he managed to make me feel safe—to make me feel like I could trust him.

"Ya know, all I've ever wanted was to love someone unconditionally and for that someone to love me back equally. My entire life I chased after that dream. My mother had let me down, my father had walked out…I never felt like it was something that I deserved. Maybe if I was a better child my mother wouldn't have turned to the drugs and alcohol. Maybe if I did my homework and didn't talk back, my father wouldn't have turned his back on us and walked out."

I could hear Lee sigh loudly in the background. "*You* are not the reason you had such a shitty upbringing. You need to learn to stop blaming yourself. Stop taking their mistakes out on your body!"

No one had ever been that blunt with me about it. I remember Travis had tried, but I hadn't been ready to hear him out—but I heard Lee loud and clear.

"I have one more question before I let you get some sleep," Lee said softly then.

"Okay."

"Do you love me?" He asked, cockily.

"Of course not, you ass!" I retorted quickly.

Lee chuckled loudly. "You're going to fall so hard for me—you're going to face plant in it," he exclaimed; I could practically picture his eyes sparkling at the crazy notion.

I giggled at the silliness of it all.

"You'll see…" He trailed off. "I'm going to be your knight in shining armor."

"Alright, goodnight Romeo."

"Goodnight Jac. Sweet dreams."

I rolled over after hanging up the phone and buried my face in my pillow. I didn't let it on then, but I was already beyond infatuated with Lee. Our phone calls had become a nightly ritual and it was rare if they were shorter than an hour or two.
Sometimes he would call me and we would each turn on the same Pandora stations and

simply listen to the music; he said it made him feel closer to me, even if we sat on the phone saying nothing, yet listening to the same music—I felt it too.

I had confided in him about a few things that were very personal to me and he still called back the following day. Something had changed about him...there was something deeper driving him now. He was persistent...It was sexy. I loved the feeling of being chased.

He had no idea I was basically eating out of the palms of his hands. He had no idea how strongly my inner feelings had developed for him over the past few weeks. One more push and he would have had me...all of me. My feelings consumed me; he consumed me.

Twenty – A Shock to the Heart

Lee

We had been conversing back and forth on good terms for a little over a month and a half, and I could feel a trust forming; feelings growing stronger by the day.

Even though Jacqueline and I were in completely different states, we kept it interesting by talking on multiple platforms— Facebook, texts, calls, and even Skype.

It didn't take me long to realize that I didn't want anyone else.

No, she wasn't perfect; in fact, she was probably the furthest thing from it, but in a way it made her more endearing. The idea that I could help her significantly improve her life was a high of its own.

"You should come visit me in Hawaii," I suggested one day on the phone, during one of our hour long conversations.

"You know how I feel about flying," Jacqueline sighed, defeated then.

"Well you know how much it scares me to pursue this…us—but I am jumping in head first; facing my fears."

"It's not the same," her tone was dejected.

"Yes it is!" I exclaimed huffily. "It's exactly the same thing. Do something that terrifies you for once in your life Jac, the outcome may surprise you."

She sighed long and hard, then silence filled the air.

"I'm *terrified* to go visit my mom in jail; I'm *terrified* of what she will have to say."

"Jac…" I began but she continued talking.

"I always thought Travis was going to be the one to go with me—the one to hold my hand the entire way through—the one to give me the courage to face her."

It was frustrating when she brought up Travis—it was hard to compete with a lifelong best friend who had never wronged her. I never felt like I stacked up. In some ways I worried that Travis had always been the one for her but she settled for a lost cause like me.

"I don't think I can do it...I don't think I can face her alone."

"I'll go with you," I said simply.

"What?"

"I said, I'll go with you," I repeated.

"Are you serious?" Her voice raised in pitch, a cute nervous trait I had noticed she carried.

"Yeah, on one condition. After I fly out to Montana and help you face your mother, you will fly back with me to Hawaii for a week." It seemed like a decent trade.

"Lee..." she began to speak but I cut her off.

"No excuses Jac, it's time to really begin living your life. Let me show you a whole new world." Okay—sometimes I could be a cheeseball. I knew I had made some sort of progress when I heard her chuckle at my Disney reference.

"I have no money saved up Lee."

"Let me take care of that. You just worry about mentally preparing yourself for all that is about to come."

"Alright Aladdin," she said so softly I had to strain to hear it.

"What was that?" I pressed.

"I said—deal."

My call waiting began beeping unexpectedly then. I glanced at the screen of my phone.

Dad.

I hadn't spoken to my father in a few months. We never had a terribly close relationship.

"Jac, can I call you back? My Dad is on the other line."

"Oh yeah. Of course." She clicked off without a goodbye.

I switched to the other line and pressed the green answer button.

"Hello?"

My father's voice sounded rough; hoarse. "Hello Lee."

"Hey Dad, what's up?" I glanced at the clock quickly noting the conversation would probably last no more than five minutes—plenty of time for me to call Jacqueline back before she would need to go to bed.

"I don't know any other way to say this than to just say it…" he trailed off.

"Whatever it is, just say it." My heart was hammering against my chest with each second that passed.

"They found your mother's remains at Titan Park, underneath some shrubs and bushes along the hiking trail."

It felt like my ears were ringing and I wasn't even sure I fully comprehended his words.

They found mom? I swallowed loudly, blinking back tears. "What happened?"

"They were investigating a string of murders that began ten years ago and they are still finding patterns—they think it is a serial killer; one they are deeply investigating. They said your mothers wounds were very similar to the other remains they have found all over Oakland, San Francisco, and even Berkley.

I wasn't sure how to respond. She hadn't left us—she had been murdered.

Guilt weighed heavily on my heart knowing I ever entertained the idea that we weren't good enough and that's why she split.

A single tear ran down my cheek slowly. "Thank you for the call." I hadn't meant to be so stiff or formal, but our relationship was only used to it.

"You're welcome—I figured it would help you stop blaming me." His tone sounded so sad, I almost felt bad for the past seven years.

"I never blamed you…I just wanted you to try harder to find her…I was a teenager, I needed her."

"I never stopped looking for her Lee, I never stopped researching. I need you to know that."

"What are you talking about?"

He cleared his throat. "I have been in contact with the police since her disappearance, I just kept it to myself because I didn't want to get your hopes up—shatter your dreams. Like you said, you were a teenager…I wanted to wait to discuss any of my ideas or theories with you until I knew you could handle it."

His confession made me angry. I could have been helping with the search for my mother from the very beginning. Maybe if I had, we would have found out the truth earlier.

"I don't think that was your choice to make." The venom in my voice was more than apparent.

"Look I'm sorry for the decisions I made in the past, but I can't go back and change them."

"No, you can't." I hung up the phone then, tossing it across the room.

I threw my head into my hands and cried for the fifteen year old me who had blamed his mother for walking out and leaving her family. I cried for the present me who was coming to terms that he would never see his mother again…something that had always been my biggest fear.

When would losing people you loved get any easier?

Twenty One – Unfair Circumstances

Jacqueline

The lights and sirens would have been alarming to anyone else…but I am different.

'What has she gotten into now?'

I pick up my pace towards my front door taking note of the police officers scattered about.

'Maybe she was caught stealing again?'

As soon as I step through my front door, I drop my backpack immediately at the sight of my mother in handcuffs.

"Umm, excuse me officers," my voice comes out shaky and high-pitched. "Can I ask what she has done?"

The portly looking man turns his gaze on me. "Oh Rebecca, you didn't tell me you had a daughter."

My stomach sinks. Something isn't right. Where's the normal warning?

"Is she going to jail?" I ask another question, hoping for an answer this time.

"Sweetheart, I think we need to take you down to the station—where we can have a talk."

Again my stomach dips.

"Why won't you tell me anything?" I'm surprised at the fear rising within my voice.

"What's your name sweetheart?" His tone remains calm and his eyes kind.

"Jacqueline," I hear my mother answer for me.

"Jacqueline, that's a beautiful name." He addresses me softly.

"Thank you." My reply comes out just as soft.

"Your mother was in the wrong place at the wrong time. Do you understand what I am saying?" The officer asks.

I shrug lightly. "Does this have to do with drugs?"

He sighs loudly then; nodding his head.

"Will you let her come home after you question her?"

The officer shakes his head no. "Your mother is facing a bit of time, I'm afraid."

"What does that mean?" I'm only twelve years old. Mature for my age, yes—but still in middle school. My mother is the only family I have around.

"Jacqueline, I'm going to need to ask you to come back to the station with me. We will finish our conversation there."

I want to scream—yell—cry—laugh—kick—punch, but instead I follow the officer without another word.

I can't even look at my mother. She did this and I am not sure I can ever forgive her.

*   *   *

The last time I had seen my mother was her trial; the one where she was sentenced to three years in prison for prostitution, drug distribution, and child endangerment.

I was immediately thrown into foster care after her sentence, for which I remained only a few years before filing for emancipation.

My mother never wrote—she never called. I followed suit. I figured if she ever wanted she could easily find me.

"It's going to be okay you know." Lee squeezed my hand from the passenger seat. "Take a deep breath." I heard him instruct.

I looked away before briefly closing my eyes and inhaling deeply.

"Do you feel better?" Lee was staring at me intently, and I on the road.

"No," I laughed nervously. "It's okay, I'm just appreciative that you are here with me."

He had kept his word to accompany me to the meeting with my mother if I agreed to a Hawaii visit immediately following.

We had arrived; I put the car in park, still breathing deeply. I heard Lee unbuckle his seatbelt, then felt him release mine.

"Jac, look at me." He gently turned my face towards his. "I'm here and I'm not going anywhere. There's nothing to fear."

I kissed him before he could even blink, taking him by surprise.

"Thank you," I whispered breathlessly between kisses.

"You ready?" Lee looked over at me, awaiting my instruction.

I nodded before reaching for the handle.

*   *   *

Orange and dull grey. The colors overtook my vision as the prisoners filed into the meeting room.

My heart rate immediately began to race and I felt Lee squeeze my hand softly reminding me that I wasn't alone; calming me down a bit.

How he could read my emotions so quickly was entrancing.

I saw her long, wavy blond hair come through first, but it looked thin; she looked thin.

I could see her bones clearly through her thin layer of skin, then my eyes locked with hers. They were sunken in and dull looking. She looked the definition of terrible.

"Jacquie baby!" She exclaimed rushing at me, her arms outstretched.

I allowed her to hug me but didn't return the embrace.

She released me then stared me up and down. "My baby is all grown up!"

I watched as she digested that thought.

"Hey, I'm Lee," I heard his deep voice interrupt.

My mother looked at me and then back to Lee, smiling widely. "Rebecca. I'm sorry that was rude of me. You're Jacquie's boyfriend right?"

I blushed when she said the word, knowing Lee would probably interject to correct her; let her know we were just good friends.

When he didn't say anything to combat her question but instead nodded lightly, I couldn't help but smile.

"So, how have you been? Have you been good?" My mother asked then.

I shrugged. "I've been as good as I could be. I've survived."

"Oh baby, I'm so sorry." Her head fell into her hands dramatically. "I'm sorry for everything. Please forgive me."

I watched as what seemed like real, genuine tears fell down her face. Without realizing what

I was doing, I reached for her hands. "I was a little girl. Scared and alone. Why didn't you ever call? Write? You have no idea the hell I went through after you."

"I made a lot of mistakes baby," She got in between sobs. "I did a lot of things I wasn't proud of because of my addictions."

Unconsciously tears began to stream down my cheeks as well.

"Baby, I *want* you to forgive me. I *need* you to forgive me. I can't let you leave here without that."

I quickly glanced at her through wet lashes. "What are you trying to say?"

"Jacqueline, I have HIV—AIDS, and I'm dying. Please just give me this one thing and I'll never ask you to come here again."

My stomach was instantly in knots. She was dying of AIDS? My eyes scanned her body again hoping it was a lie. But there was no question she was telling the truth; she looked like death.

"How long do you have?" I choked out, feeling Lee's hand on my knee as support.

"The doc said I have less than six months, but other than that, he couldn't be more specific." Even her voice came out drained like she appeared to be.

I had resented my mother for as long as I could remember for forcing me to grow up faster than I was ready, but somewhere, hidden deep down inside, was the young girl naïve enough to think her mother could change. The girl who believed her mother would come save her from the evils of the world...but she never came.

Even after her first stint in jail, I held out hope that she would find me and move me into a house with her where magically everything was going to be better...but it wasn't.

Travis's father was a deputy and no more than a week after her release, he picked her up for another drug and prostitution charge.

Eventually I just gave up any hope that I would *ever* see or hear from her again. But even after all of the crap I had been through, I still wanted a mother.

How many times I had only wished my mother would get what she deserved—but death had never crossed my mind.

*　　*　　*

The fresh air was exactly what I needed. As soon as I was out of the dark, dreary building I fell to my knees inhaling sharply.

"Well I didn't see that one coming," Lee joked, attempting to lighten the situation.

"Lee…" I could barely get out.

He was at my side in an instant helping me up.

"Thank you," I choked out and then proceeded to drench his shoulder with tears; sobbing uncontrollably.

Twenty Two – Pillar of Support

Lee

She had been broken. Now she was destroyed. I knew what this could do to her; would do to her. I couldn't sit back and do nothing—so I gave her tough love.

"Where are they?" I asked as I turned on the bathroom lights.

"Excuse me?" She pretended to be puzzled by my question.

"Don't play dumb—you know exactly what I am talking about." I remained stiff.

Jacqueline sighed loudly before pushing past me into the small room. She glanced back at me warily. "Well are you just going to stand there eyeing me down like I'm some kind of criminal?"

"I'm not taking my eyes off you for a second," I replied simply.

"Are you saying you don't trust me?" She asked incredulously, her jaw dropping open in a surprised fashion.

"Damn straight."

I heard her groan loudly then watched as she began to open her cabinet hidden behind her mirror.

Slowly she reached in and then handed me a razor, not even able to look me in the eyes.

"There, you happy?"

I shook my head no. "Where are the others?"

"There aren't any others—that was it." Her words felt like venom to me.

"Yeah, and my name is Adolf Hitler." I yawned. "The others?" My hand remained extended until two more razors magically appeared. I was surprised. I had been so sure she was going to put up more of a fight.

I chucked all three blades without another thought. Hidden deep inside a dumpster on the street I was positive Jacqueline would never think to look.

Tears began streaming down her face as I returned. "You don't know anything about me; how I handle my pain or my grief!"

"I don't know a lot..." I paused. "I'll admit that, but what I know is you're a riddle I want to solve. A puzzle I want to piece together."

I needed to open her eyes. I needed her to understand I wasn't going anywhere. I needed to reintroduce her to vulnerability.

"Do you want to talk about what happened back there?" I asked softly.

"Leave me alone!" She growled turning her back to me.

I grabbed for her but she shook me off violently.

"Jac, come here." I attempted to keep my voice soothing.

She stopped so I took the initiative to inch closer.

What I hadn't been anticipating? A rough slap across the cheek; one you could probably hear in China.

I reached up to massage my sore cheek. What the hell was with women and slapping me? Was I really such a terrible scumbag?

Jacqueline's facial expression was a mix of sheer horror and embarrassment. "Oh my God!" She shrieked, throwing her hands over her mouth. "I don't know what I was thinking."

"It's okay," I found myself saying out of habit.

"No, it's not okay." She began choking up and threw her arms around my neck.

Her body was shaking from her heavy tears. I stroked her hair softly, not saying a word.

After her wails had died down into sniffles and deep breaths, I finally felt compelled to say something. "This isn't your fault you know."

I felt her body shift from my words.

I quickly ran to grab her tissues.

"Your mother made her own choices; she was selfish. It wasn't your fault that she couldn't see your worth until it was too late." I handed her a couple tissues then moved a strand of hair out of her eyes.

Even in her current state she was still breathtakingly beautiful.

"I'm fucked up," Jacqueline said softly after delicately wiping away her tears.

"Me too," I replied, inching closer.

"Why would you ever want to waste your time on someone like me?" She asked in an insecure tone.

"Because for the first time in my life, in as long as I can remember, I have faith. *You* make me a believer."

She closed the final distance between us and then allowed me to kiss her.

I knew she was still hurting, and I had no intention of taking advantage of her in such a fragile state so I broke the kiss quickly and then led her to her bedroom.

In no time at all we were curled up together on her bed. I could hear her steady breathing as she drifted off to sleep.

Jacqueline

He hasn't left my side in a week. I thought for sure he would have run—hopped the first red eye out of here, but his handsome face was what I awoke to every morning, what I fell asleep to every night.

He was becoming part of my routine.

"I don't know how I'm going to pay rent," I muttered into my pillow.

"I took care of it," he answered.

"What are you talking about?" I asked, sitting straight up.

"I said, I took care of it. Now, call Travis's mom back and tell her that you won't be coming back to work."

"Lee, that's my only income. They've been like family to me. I don't want to burn every bridge…" I looked at him, desperate for direction.

"Do you trust me?" Lee asked.

I thought about it for a second. I could count the people I had trusted in my life on one hand,

Parker and Travis easily made that list, and oddly enough, Lee. With all of our correspondence over the months, we had really gotten to know one another on a deeper level. I nodded.

"Then come back with me to Hawaii. Quit your job, leave your small apartment behind and embrace change; embrace the unknown."

I giggled. I'd be stupid to pass this up. He saw all of me and accepted it. He saw me go from zero to one hundred and didn't write me off then.

Oddly enough, he hadn't been scared away yet and I needed to capitalize on that.

"Okay."

"Okay what?"

"Okay, I'll go to Hawaii with you…" He attacked me with his lips then.

"Good answer," he managed to get out between kisses.

Twenty Three – Vulnerability Woes

Lee

"What are you doing? Are you holding your breath?" I exclaimed; Jacqueline's face was growing a deeper shade by the moment and it was making me nervous. "I said deep breaths, not *no* breath!"

I exhaled a sigh of relief in unison with hers. "I'm here." I patted her knee softly.

"Um, Stewardess?" I called to the flight attendant at the front of the plane—not four feet away as we were sitting in first class. "Can we get some liquid courage?"

"Sure thing tiger," she replied animatedly. "What's your drug of choice?"

"Can I get two vodkas for the lady…" I began when Jacqueline nudged me hard with her shoulder.

"Something stronger," she choked out, her eyes still tightly closed.

175

"Uh, actually, can we make that four fun sized bottles of your finest whiskey and a soda to chase it with?"

The flight attendant pulled out a bottle of Coca-Cola. "Coke fine?"

I nodded my head, taking note that Jacqueline's head was basically in her lap.

I paid for our drinks and then Jacqueline finally spoke. "I think I'm going to be sick!"

I swallowed hoping I could get her mind off of it. "It's all mental Jac, we haven't even left the ground. They haven't even closed the cabin door yet...don't you think you're being a bit dramatic?"

She looked back like she was going to strangle me. "You think I'm overreacting, is that it?"

So I had successfully taken her mind off of her puking, but I had pissed her off in the process.

"Cheers." I clinked glasses with hers and took a swig off of my whiskey and coke.

She looked at me with a shocked expression.

"Are you just going to let me get away with it— or are you going to catch up?" I challenged her

176

playfully. I didn't have to wait for an answer—
she was downing her cocktail instantly.

"Liquid courage." She clinked her glass against
mine before downing it all in one long gulp.

"Damn," I replied to her ballsy move.

When Jacqueline had actually kept her promise
of coming back to Hawaii with me, I was
beyond surprised and happy, but I knew her
first flying experience wasn't going to be a cake
walk.

Two bottles deep and Jacqueline was excited
rather than nervous. The liquid courage had
worked its magic—or so I thought, until take
off when she basically crushed my hand in half
from her death grip, or the bit of turbulence we
had when she let out her loud yelps and cries.

All in all, I was happy to break her into flying.
If we worked out, she was going to have to
learn to love traveling and long flights.

By the third bottle she was out like a light bulb,
passed out on my shoulder quietly snoring and
even drooling a little.

She looked adorable. I couldn't move a muscle
for fear of waking her. So when we finally

landed and she came to, my shoulder was numb.

"You survived your first flight—do tell, how are you feeling?" I teaser her.

Jacqueline blinked her eyes a few times, attempting to wake herself up. "We're here?"

"Yup."

"Already? And you let me sleep through it? You jerk!" She punched me softly in the shoulder but it felt like a solid blow because of the earlier soreness.

I rolled it gingerly back and forth.

"You okay?" She asked naively.

I chuckled lightly as I reached into the overhead bin to grab our bags. "I may need a massage later." I wiggled my eyebrows at her as we waited to de-plane.

"Okay," she replied simply, surprising the hell out of me. "What? You've done a lot for me…it's the least I can do."

I was stunned to silence. I just stared at her like she had two heads. "Okay, who are you and what did you do with my girlfriend?"

I knew my statement would surprise her. I wanted to see her genuine response to me putting a label on whatever we had been doing the past few weeks.

"Girlfriend?" She asked, glancing back at me as we exited the plane and headed out of the airport.

"Well, wouldn't that be an accurate description for what we've been doing? I mean, we have been practically gallivanting around like an old married couple—living together for the past few weeks and all..." I trailed off.

Jacqueline dropped her luggage and came charging at me. She hopped into my arms and as I held her there, suspended in air, our lips met each other's in a passionate encounter.

"Take me home," she gasped between kisses and you better bet I obeyed with no time to waste.

Jacqueline

I had thought the first time was passionate...the second time was record breaking. We had barely made it through his front door when our luggage hit the floor with a bang and Lee had literally scooped me up in his arms, carrying me to his bedroom.

Even though we had been cohabitating for close to three weeks, Lee had been a complete and utter gentleman; sticking to the plan of taking it slow…especially after my mother's confession.

His shirt was off within seconds. I couldn't help it, his abs turned me on like no other.

He pulled my shirt down, exposing my shoulder. He kissed it passionately then, before pulling the entire shirt off and tossing it onto the ground beneath us. He laid me on the bed then in my bra and jeans, holding my arms above my head as he continued to trail my neck with kisses.

My breathing had deepened; my inner thighs growing hotter. His hands were exploring every inch of my body, causing me to tremble out with pleasure.

"Wait!" I called out, exasperated.

"What is it?" Lee jerked upright.

"I promised you a massage." I proceeded to stand up and order him face down on the bed.

"Right now?" Lee asked, glancing down at his obvious erection.

"Lay down," I ordered sternly.

"Yes ma'am!" Lee spun around and face-planted into his king sized bed.

I giggled before hopping on top of him. I began with working out some of the tension I felt along his lower back and upper shoulder blades. His body was beyond perfect—like a sculpture I was nervous of breaking.

I was kissing the area between his shoulder blades when he maneuvered himself back on top of me, pressing down into me so I could feel his erect penis.

I kissed him quickly before allowing him to remove my bra letting my breasts topple out.

"God, you are so sexy," he whispered before taking of my breasts in his mouth and torturing me little by little.

The foreplay was so spot on I had him seconds from pleasure before he finally entered me and I felt the rough, fiery feeling between my legs. It felt hot, it felt good, and it felt right.

That was until he reached for my knee high socks to begin removing them. I grabbed at his hands to stop him. "What do you think you're doing?"

"I'm trying to get you to be yourself with me." He kissed me gently then. "Do you trust me?"

I nodded.

"Then shut up." He smiled a devilish grin at me before kissing me passionately while removing my socks. Instantly I threw my hands to cover my scars. He was going to think I was disgusting. He was never going to want anything to do with me after he saw what I did to myself.

What I hadn't told anyone was that I hadn't touched a blade since the night he discarded all of mine; a big accomplishment for me. What would normally consume my every thought changed to a dark skinned, dark haired boy...he invaded them.

"Oh baby," he threw his hand over his mouth and I was sure I was hallucinating, but tears were welling up in his eyes.

I looked away, uncomfortable, attempting to cover up my bad mistakes.

"Why would you ever do this to yourself?" He asked, choking on his tears.

Tears unconsciously stung at the sides of my eyes at seeing a man so vulnerable. And not any man, a man I clearly cared about. I was crazy about him.

"I stopped." It was all I could muster up.

"When?" He asked.

"July 13th."

"That was…" Lee trailed off as he began to put it all together.

"Being with you has been my medicine," I said, a silent tear running its course down my cheek.

Lee lowered his lips to mine and kissed me deeply and passionately. I tugged gently on his bottom lip playfully. And even though we were a snotty mess, our kisses had never felt deeper, more in sync. Our bodies had never mirrored each other's so perfectly before.

Nothing was off limits…the ground, the bed, or a chair—we tried it all.

The sexiest thing about him was his ability to go and then go again and then go again. I swear he wore me out.

After I went to the bathroom to clean myself up and searched for a pair of pajamas...only to realize I had forgotten to pack any, Lee had carefully laid out a pair of his nerdy holiday boxers and a short sleeved white shirt.

After slipping on the oversized pajamas he had picked out for me, I climbed into his bed where he was sleeping soundly and wrapped my arms around him from behind. He flinched. I was pretty positive he felt it. And then I closed my eyes as well, breathing in every bit of him.

God damn him.

I was face-planting. I had lost my balance. He caught me off guard—I let down my walls for him. If he even knew he held my world in his hands I wondered how he would react. Would he run? Why could I read so many other people in my life—but not Lee?

Take Travis for example. I knew he loved me. I knew he wanted to be more than friends since day one. I just pretended to stay clueless and ignore the fact. The less attention I gave it, the better.

But Lee had been so unpredictable from day one. It was the thing I found irresistible and frustrating about him all at the same time. I had been afraid to admit it, especially to myself, but he was right, it wouldn't be long before there was no turning back.

Twenty Four – Insecurities Have no Place Here

Lee

She had entered my world. One immersed with family, adventure, fear, and loyalty. I wasn't sure she knew what she had signed up for, but she had been an unnaturally good sport lately, and as much as I wanted to believe her when she said I was her medicine, I still worried—I still wanted to be prepared.

After a long, hot shower I stepped into my favorite robe and sat down on the bed next to her. She looked so peaceful. I gently swept a few hairs out of her face. She stirred when I did it.

"You've got to be joking me…" she muttered through one cracked eye.

"Rise and shine," I said softly; this was the girl I had been expecting.

"Austyn and Avery are going to be here in less than an hour. We're picking them up from the airport."

"What?" Jacqueline choked out. "Your cousin?"

"And her boyfriend, yes. So you're going to want to get ready."

I heard a loud groan come out of her little body.

"Five more minutes!" She exclaimed then disappeared back underneath the covers. I laughed lightly, letting her get her way.

Thirty minutes later and Jacqueline hadn't moved a muscle. In fact, she was still fast asleep. I ended up having to pick up the pair by my lonesome. I had to wonder if it was a coincidence or not…if Jacqueline was actually asleep or pretending to be so she could avoid the situation altogether.

"So, where is she?" Austyn began looking around the car animatedly.

"Well, she's definitely not under the seats or in the trunk—so my best guess would be back at my place." I chuckled at my lame joke.

Austyn punched me in the shoulder playfully. "Don't be an ass."

"She's still sleeping."

Austyn let up finally. "Awww, poor girl. Did you two have a late night?"

"You're disgusting if you think I'd discuss my sex life with you."

"Rude!" Austyn shrieked. "I missed you."

"Back at ya cuz," I bared my pearly whites at her.

"So Avery, you ready for some adventures?" I finally acknowledged my pal sitting in the backseat.

"Yeah man, what do you have in mind?"

"Jac's never been surfing, snorkeling, or zip lining…your pick."

"Fuck yeah!" I saw Avery's eyes light up in my rearview mirror.

As we pulled into the driveway I worried that Jacqueline was still going to be passed out. "Jacqueline may still be sleeping so let's try to keep it down."

"Oh Lee…" I heard Austyn gush.

I looked over at her quickly. "Don't start."

She threw her hands over her mouth like she was attempting to hold in a best kept secret.

"I'm just being a nice host," I said.

After leaving Austyn and Avery in my living room I headed for my own bedroom; the last place I had left Jacqueline. I opened the door softly, but was surprised to see the bed was empty.

I closed my bedroom door behind me and headed for my bathroom, opening the door. Instantly I heard the familiar pelts of water against glass.

Jacqueline was taking a shower. Even though I had seen her naked multiple times before, I was still a gentleman—so I averted my eyes. "You okay?"

"Lee?"

I closed the bathroom door behind me, inching closer to her voice, still averting my eyes.

"Austyn and Avery are here."

"Why do you want me to meet them?" She asked from inside the glass case.

"Because I care about you and I want to introduce you to other people I care about." Why was she questioning any of it? She had signed up for a fresh start, yet seemed hesitant.

"I'm coming closer," I warned as I stepped towards the shower. I could now clearly see through the fog enough to know that Jacqueline was sitting on the ground of the shower—her knees pulled up under her chin and her arms wrapped around them. "What are you doing?" I asked softly.

"What if they hate me? What if they see my true colors one night and they convince you to leave me?" Her insecurities were sky high.

"It won't happen," I replied without hesitation. "They are going to love you."

"You know that's not true." Jacqueline laughed softly.

"But did it make you feel better?"

She nodded.

"Then my job here is done. Now let's get you dried off." I opened up the glass door and reached for the silver knobs turning off the water.

I grabbed her towel off the back of the door and then held it wide open. This time I didn't look away, I savored every bit of the woman walking towards me.

It was happening. I hadn't paid it much attention in the beginning but I was headed to the point of no return. My days began to revolve around one thing, or rather one person who was all I worried about. She was slowly becoming the most important person in my life and it was terrifying the hell out of me.

I knew deep down what I was feeling, I just wasn't sure I was prepared to face the truth head on yet.

Twenty Five – Zero to Sixty, You in or You Out?

Jacqueline

I had never grinded my teeth together harder or been more terrified in my life. The old Jacqueline would have had a full on melt-down; a psychotic episode, but I was holding my poker face rather well.

Inside, I was shaking like a scared little girl. The only thing that was even keeping me sane was Lee's tight, comforting grip on my knee.

I looked up into his eyes and without saying a word he instantly made me feel calmer. He was looking at me as if to say, 'it's going to be okay, I'm here'…and I believed every word.

"We're close," one of the instructors said then.

I glanced to my right where Austyn and Avery were seated.

Earlier Austyn had been really excited for our adventure—but now she appeared quiet and timid.

Avery looked the epitome of calm, cool, and collected. I remembered him telling me he had gone skydiving before—so this little outing was more exhilarating for him and Lee because they knew what to expect.

Us newbies drowned in maybe's and what if's. We were women after all...

"I'll go if you go." I wasn't sure where it came from—but I meant every word of it.

I could sense Austyn's hesitation from a mile away, but I thought the notion of us both being novices would be appealing.

Austyn looked at me, not saying anything, just staring.

"We're going to do this girl, and we're going to fucking love it," she said finally in a matter-of-fact tone.

Lee broke out into a wide grin, and then they announced it was time.

My heart began to race faster; Lee squeezed my knee harder. It was real—it was actually happening.

They opened up the door, and Avery along with his instructor, were out of the plane in minutes

My heart was pounding loudly in my ears.

"Skydiving—really?" I turned to address Lee with my question.

"Now? You ask this now?" Lee was glancing between me and our awaiting instructors.

"Yeah," I answered simply.

"It was all or nothing. We can work our way backwards to the easier victories—but if you can do this, you can do anything."

I had to give it to him, his speech wasn't half bad.

"Let's do this Austyn," I turned to my right.

She nodded her head slowly, standing.

I turned back to Lee and kissed him slowly and passionately, enjoying every second of it.

I felt his hands reach the back of my neck; we both let ourselves get lost in the kiss.

When I pulled away, I looked around for Austyn and noticed she was moments from making the leap.

"Austyn!" I called out loudly so she could hear me.

She shifted her gaze to me instantly.

"See ya down there."

She smiled then before jumping. I gasped at the suddenness of it.

Lee grabbed my hand and gave it a tight squeeze. "We are going to do this together. I am right behind you babe."

I took a deep breath and digested his words as our instructors linked up to us so we could make the plunge. We were the last two pairs on the plane.

As soon as I saw how high we were and felt the wind slap my face, I felt frozen in fear.

I'm right behind you, Lee's words played on repeat in the back of my head.

"You ready?" My instructor shouted over my shoulder.

I nodded, not even believing myself. It all happened in the blink of an eye. My stomach lurched forward as my feet lost their balance and suddenly I was free falling.

I never got the chance to tell him that I loved him.

* * *

Skydiving. It happened. It was eye opening; life changing.

After my rough landing, I glanced up at the never-ending sky searching for a glimpse of my boyfriend.

Boyfriend. Lee was *my* boyfriend. Lee accepted *me.*

I love him.

"There!" My instructor pointed to his left about a half mile away.

Sure enough, I could see Lee's dark skin and blue parachute from where we were standing.

I looked at my surroundings for any sight of Austyn or Avery and noticed the lip-locked pair a few yards away.

I smiled quickly then turned towards the general area I had seen Lee moments earlier.

I was going after *my man*.

*   *   *

Austyn and Avery didn't stay much longer. Just long enough for them to experience my first surfing experience.

I couldn't stand up on the board to save my life, I swallowed way too much salt water, and I left with a pretty bad sunburn.

They were everything Lee had made them out to be—and more. I loved the dynamic of their relationship and I envied how easily they solved their problems. They were a beautiful couple.

I was able to semi-hold my composure their entire visit, definitely something to be proud of.

Austyn and Lee's relationship was admirable—this unbreakable bond you couldn't see, but could feel. They loved spending time together and I loved how much of a positive role model she was to him…Avery as well.

Having the time to see the interaction between Lee and his cousin and friend only made me fall deeper in love with him. I almost blurted it out a few times…but I wanted him to be the first one to say it—I was old fashioned in that way.

But I could see how much he cared about me in his voice; his demeanor; his affection. He was whipped and he had no clue.

Twenty Six – Grounded and Digging it

Lee

Jacqueline probably hated me, but I was breaking her out of her shell slowly—she probably didn't even realize how much she had changed.

She still had her bad days. The ones she went from zero to sixty in ten seconds flat, but if I was around, I could calm her down in the matter of a few minutes.

She tried to mask the effect I had on her, but it was obvious—I made her better. I also think by introducing her to new things and opening her eyes, she was slowly beginning to heal some old scars.

It was 6:00 pm on a Sunday night and I had lured Jacqueline into the car with me for a rendezvous.

"Where are we going?" Jacqueline asked from the passenger seat.

I glanced over at her quickly, then back on the road. "You don't know how to swim—I am going to teach you."

"Lee, I don't have my swimsuit…" Jacqueline trailed off.

I glanced in the rearview mirror at the backseat noting not only my swim suit, but also one I had bought for her.

"I've got it covered," I replied finally.

Jacqueline stared at me awaiting an explanation.

"Look, it's not that big of a deal, but I had Austyn help me pick one out for you when she was in town—hopefully we did well…"

"I'm sure you guys did just fine," she said, then squeezed my arm.

We pulled up to a familiar gym I liked to frequent, the parking lot was bare minus a few cars here and there.

As we entered the front doors we were greeted by the receptionist, a younger, brown haired boy.

"Hey man," I said, exchanging handshakes with him.

"Lee, everything is ready for you."

"Thanks Jake," I replied. Then I stealthily slipped him a twenty dollar bill.

I knew how difficult it was for Jacqueline to show her legs to anyone and I knew how much I cared about her so I did a buyout of the gym for the day. It actually wasn't as expensive as I would have thought. They gave me a huge discount for all the business I gave them through my client referrals. I ended up dropping $10,000 to keep the gym closed for three hours. It was worth it.

After we changed in the locker rooms, we emerged and I couldn't stop staring at Jacqueline. Austyn had chosen the tankini, whatever that was and Jacqueline looked beautiful. Austyn had been spot on.

We started off in the shallow end. That way she could touch the ground, in turn feeling safe.

I initiated a water fight to make her feel even more secure. I had never seen her smile more.

"Okay, I'm going to need you to lie flat on your back, I'm going to teach you how to float." Instinctively, I put my arms out in front of me.

I felt Jacqueline's weightless body fall back onto my arms and I guided her around the pool. When we had been in the deep end for more than ten minutes, I removed my arms from underneath Jacqueline. Her eyes were closed and by the time she realized she was alone, I was already halfway across the pool.

"Lee?" She began to kick her legs, flailing her arms, looking for me; causing her to accidentally swallow some pool water.

"Jac, I'm right here," I said in a calming voice. "You were doing fine until you began second guessing yourself. Just kick your feet underneath you and keep your head above water."

I swam out to her after I saw a visible change in her posture. "How you doing?"

"You're an ass, but I'm swimming!"

"Now that's the spirit!" I wiggled my eyebrows at her.

She wrapped her legs around my torso. "Don't leave me again," she murmured.

"I'm not going anywhere." Jacqueline was my life now. I spent every waking moment apart from work wrapped up in her.

For once in my life someone had grounded me—and I liked it.

"What are you thinking about?" Jacqueline ran her fingers gently over my forehead.

"You," I replied, honestly.

Her eyes grew wide. "What about me?"

"You've managed to ground me; this is the longest I've been in one single place in years."

Jacqueline looked enthused. "That's awesome."

"That's awesome? That's all you have to say after I made that huge confession?" She was being modest.

"I knew you liked me more than you let on...I've just been waiting for you to come out and say it!" She poked me in the chest playfully.

"Oh really? I'm going to drop you in this water!" I tried to release her limbs from my body but they were hanging on for dear life.

I couldn't help but laugh. This was us. Jacqueline was my girlfriend and I was falling hard. If I didn't watch it I would be the one face planting in love with her much quicker than I had ever anticipated.

My player days were being put behind me and I felt relieved; I felt renewed.

Twenty Seven – An Unexpected Visitor

Jacqueline

Jealousy did not suit me. I did not wear it well.

In all reality, I felt pretty secure in my relationship with Lee but seeing the brunette bimbo with huge boobs at his front door had me spinning.

"Is Lee home?" She asked in a high-pitched Barbie sounding voice. She had brown eyes and they lit up when she said his name.

There was definite history between the two. I thought she might get the hint seeing that I answered the door in my pajamas—but then again she didn't seem fazed.

"Lee is out on his morning surf, want me to let him know you stopped by?"

The brunette's face dropped in disappointment. "Yeah, could you just tell him Ainsley stopped by?

Ainsley. Ainsley. Lee had never mentioned her name before—maybe she was just a friend? Wishful thinking.

As soon as she made her exit I hopped onto the computer, quickly stalking Lee's Facebook.

I was going to snoop and find out exactly who Ainsley was to Lee. Her page was an easy find through his friends list.

The first thing I clicked on was her pictures. Ainsley looked so happy; her pictures portrayed a very positive, outgoing person.

It wasn't difficult to locate old pictures of her and Lee. There were entire albums named after the pair—it would be safe to say their history exceeded my expectations.

There were pictures of them kissing from nearly four years ago and obviously while Lee was still in college.

He had longer, shaggy hair back then—something I was thankful he had opted out of by shaving his head.

Judging by the dates on the pictures, they had dated for over a year, making me wonder how serious they had become—Lee had never been big on commitment, especially because it made him vulnerable..I had to wonder how close he had let Ainsley in.

Their pictures were perfect...almost too perfect. It made me question why it didn't work out.

Chicago, Illinois.

At least I knew she was only visiting Hawaii. But the fact that they mirrored a perfect couple and the knowledge that Ainsley was probably more put together than me, made me nervous.

What did she want? Why did she seek him out after all this time?

I hadn't realized just how long I had sat there— staring at an old picture of the two; the happy couple, but I hadn't moved a muscle when Lee walked through his door, his wet suit hanging off his body.

"Babe, the waves were incredible today!" He stated as he walked through the door carrying his board.

My eyes were still fixated on the screen. When I didn't respond, Lee made his way further into his place, inching towards me. "What are you doing?"

I could feel his breath on the back of my neck sending chills down my spine.

"Why are you looking at a picture of me and one of my college girlfriends?" Lee dropped his board on the wood floor loudly.

"Oh, you mean Ainsley? Maybe because she randomly stopped by earlier." I couldn't help the stiffness in my voice—I still wanted to know what her motives were.

"Ainsley showed up here?" Lee's face mirrored his shocked vocal response.

I nodded, my heart beating out of my chest ferociously. "What did she want Lee?"

Lee covered his mouth with his hand. "Well that was definitely unexpected…"

"What happened between you two?" I pushed for an explanation.

"She was someone I dated in college. We were semi-serious."

"What's that supposed to mean?" I asked, still digging for details.

"It means I was under the impression we were 'dating' and Ainsley was under the impression we were 'exclusive'."

"You didn't…" I trailed off, lost in thought—my jealousy slowly fading.

"I did, and in turn I really broke her heart. I haven't regretted much in my life…but what I did to Ainsley was definitely one of those moments."

I couldn't hide the disappointment that spread across my face like wildfire.

"Ainsley and I were a long time ago. I haven't even thought about her in a long time."

"Well, she's in town and wants to see you." I muttered, worst case scenarios playing out in my head on repeat.

"You mean more to me now than Ainsley ever could or even did. You should find comfort in that." Lee said softly, approaching me.

"I do. I just worry. I have so many flaws—it's easier to imagine you choosing someone else over me for a wide variety of reasons.

"Look, while I do agree you are a handful sometimes—you are still my handful—one I signed up for and intend on keeping around for a very long time, if you'll have me."

He was too good to be true—better even. What did I do to deserve such an amazing man? I wasn't sure—but I was holding on for dear life; I would not be giving up without a fight.

Twenty Eight – Caught off Guard in the Worst Way

Lee

I never thought I would ever hear the name Ainsley Townsend again…

It could have had to do with our rough break-up and falling out, or it could have been my indecisive nature when it came to being in a fully committed, monogamous relationship.

A few years after everything went sour between the two of us, I reached out to Ainsley. Call it curiosity, but I toyed with the idea that I had made a mistake—that I hadn't given Ainsley what she deserved.

Honestly she deserved someone better than me; someone willing to give her the title she was so desperately seeking. So, I cut her loose; I figured it was what would be best in the long run.

It didn't mean that she didn't cross my mind from time to time. I always hoped that she ended up with someone who would love her unconditionally; something I could never do.

When Jacqueline gave me the surprise of a lifetime by letting me know she showed up out of nowhere, my mind ran wild.

What could she possibly want after all these years?

In the spirit of not worrying Jacqueline any more than necessary, I called Ainsley's old number when I went out for my morning surf. Only this morning my focus was not on surfing—it was solely on finding out exactly what she wanted and why she was in Hawaii.

Ainsley answered on the second ring. It was surprising how familiar her voice still sounded.

"Hello?"

"Ainsley," I said, unsure of how to proceed.

"Lee," she responded, and then we just sat in silence for a couple of seconds digesting it all.

"I never thought I'd hear from you again…" I trailed off.

"Yeah, the last time I saw you I stormed off on you and a delicious meal at Lemon Drop," she recalled.

212

I tried hard to forget that night and how shitty of a person she made me feel...she pushed for commitment—but it was the time of my life, settling down was not an option.

"Oh yeah, that night..." I paused. "So how have you been—what are you doing in Hawaii?"

"I've been good, and it's kind of complicated, did you want to grab lunch and catch up?" Ainsley asked then.

I glanced at the watch on my wrist; it was a quarter after nine. "Yeah, that sounds great—let's plan to meet at noon at Le Thai Bistro."

"Sounds great—I'll see you then."

"Oh, and Ainsley, it's really great to hear your voice—you sound well," I threw in before hanging up.

I knew how Jacqueline would feel about my lunch date with my former girlfriend, so I did something I wasn't proud of; I lied.

I texted Jacqueline to let her know that a few of my clients had changed their appointments to the afternoon and I would only have time to come home and change.

I kept it as brief as possible when I made it home. Only taking twenty minutes to change and leave again. I was a terrible liar, I kept the talking to a minimum.

I arrived to Le Thai Bistro a half an hour early; spending the rest of the downtime before window shopping for flowers for Jac out of guilt.

Ainsley looked like a spitting image of her college self, brown hair, chocolate eyes—she hadn't changed one bit.

I, on the other hand, looked worlds different from when we had dated. I was in the midst of my hippie phase; let's just say it wasn't pretty.

"Lee," she said in a shocked tone.

"Is it the hair?" I joked, running my hand over my short buzz cut.

"You look good," she whispered as I embraced her for a hug.

"And you my dear look just like the woman I remember."

"I don't know if that's a good thing or a bad thing," she laughed uncomfortably.

"Familiarity is always good. You wanna sit?" I motioned towards our table.

"Sure." Ainsley took a seat at the small table across from me.

"So, first things first, what the heck are you doing in Hawaii?"

"Before that, I want to know what *you* have been doing these past four years and how you ended up in Hawaii."

Ainsley and I had met our freshman year of college at San Francisco State—previous to that I had grown up in Berkley.

"Life couldn't be better," I gushed. "I have an amazing career, an awesome house, and an incredible girlfriend."

It was true, all of it—and I was proud of all of those aspects.

It was hard to miss Ainsley's face falling with each point.

"That's great Lee, I'm so happy for you." Something told me she didn't believe her own words...

"Enough about me, your turn."

Ainsley paused before revealing anything so we could order and then we picked up the conversation exactly where we had dropped off.

"Since the last time I saw you, I got my nursing degree, became an RN, moved to Chicago, and also have someone very special in my life." She had always been incredibly smart, but I felt proud that she went after her dream.

"What's the lucky fella's name?" I asked, curiously.

"Tanner," Ainsley responded. Would you like to see a picture?"

"Sure," I answered enthusiastically. In reality, I only held a mild curiosity, but I wanted to humor her.

She handed me her phone then and I was surprised to see a picture of a young boy.

"Tanner?" I asked, glancing between the picture and Ainsley.

She nodded, remaining mute.

"He's definitely a stud, how old is he?" I asked.

"He'll be turning five this year."

Five? Five? "But that would've meant you got pregnant our freshman year of college…" I trailed off, slowly digesting it all.

She nodded.

Holy shit.

Twenty Nine – Mysterious Actions Abound

Jacqueline

Something felt different; off. From the bouquet of roses to the incredibly sweet handwritten card to his over the top affection—he was trying too hard. Not that I didn't appreciate every single moment of the special treatment, just that it was terribly suspicious.

"What is the occasion?" I found myself asking as Lee had suddenly suggested dinner as well.

"I missed you, that's all," he murmured into my neck as he pulled me into him. His breath on my neck was sending chills all throughout my body.

"You were gone for less than eight hours, are you sure you're feeling well?" I joked, pressing the back of my hand to his forehead.

Lee heaved me up and over his shoulder as I wailed from the surprise and he carried me back to our bedroom, slamming me down on the soft bed.

I was giggling from his crazy antics. "You are so weird!"

"I'll show you weird!" He threatened then began snorting into my neck. The feeling was leaving me breathless from laughing.

Then Lee stopped suddenly and just looked down at me, my body sprawled out underneath his. We were just staring into each other's eyes without a word. He ran his fingers through my hair, pulling gently at it every so often making me moan out lightly with pleasure.

He kissed me quickly then, stroking my ear while doing so.

I would never tire of his kisses. Passionate, not sloppy, and extremely sexy.

He took my bottom lip between his teeth gingerly, sucking on it.

Lee always knew exactly what moves would drive me crazy. And he always executed them expertly.

Even though his body was making all the right moves it almost felt like his head was somewhere else; a feeling I wasn't at all accustomed to.

I took his tongue between my teeth and sucked on it as if it were his dick in my mouth. I was shifting the power.

Lee was melting into me. I wasted no time ripping his shirt off and throwing it to the ground. I ran my hands over his sculpted chest, savoring the moment. His body was a temple.

I climbed on top of his lap, straddling him, kissing him passionately. My hands were running through his short hair, back and forth. He was reaching for the straps of my tank top, I didn't stop him. I was left in my bra and shorts, still straddling him and madly making out.

My phones vibration had me groaning out loud.

"Do you need to get that now?" Lee asked, irritated.

I glanced at the screen, noting that it was the prison calling. "It's my mother."

Lee stopped instantly, releasing me. "Answer it."

I reached for my phone, standing up in the process. "Hello?"

"Ms. Blunt?" An unfamiliar male voice spoke then.

"Yes…" I began, unsteady.

"This is Dr. Townsend from Montana Department of Corrections, your mother's condition has worsened and we are unsure of how much longer she has. I would recommend that you make a trip out to say your goodbyes."

My stomach sank. No. It was too soon. She said six months…it hasn't even been half that amount of time!

Lee was holding me up before I realized my legs had crumpled underneath me. "It's my mother…"

He wasted no time comforting me by taking me into his arms and stroking my hair. After I finished the phone call, I stared at Lee through tear-stricken eyes. "It's too early…it's not fair."

"I know," he responded calmly.

"I have to say goodbye," I said more to myself than Lee.

"It would be for the best."

"Will you come with me?" I asked, searching his eyes for the hero who always saved me.

Lee sighed heavily. "I need to tell you something." He took my hand in his, attempting to comfort me as he dished the news.

My stomach sank for the second time that night. Something in my gut was telling me I wasn't going to like what Lee was about to reveal.

"I met with Ainsley today…" Lee began slowly, gauging my reaction.

A pang of jealousy, hurt, and betrayal shot through my body at the mention of her name. He had snuck out to see her and lied to me about it. No wonder he had been so overly affectionate earlier—he was feeling guilty. He had tried to overcompensate. "And?" I found myself asking anxiously.

"She shared some pretty shocking news."

He was stalling…why, I wasn't quite sure. "I'm listening," I said frustrated.

"Jac, she told me that I may be a father."

I blinked repeatedly, hoping that I had heard wrong.

"Did you hear what I said?" Lee pressed.

"Please don't repeat it." I barely choked out.

"I am going to get a paternity test babe, I am going to be positive before I make any decisions." Like that was going to make anything better—my mind was racing with the countless negative outcomes.

"I need to start packing," I said, attempting to change the subject to anything less devastating.

"Jac, please stop—I'm not sure what I should do," Lee stated honestly.

"You obviously need to stay here and sort this out; I will deal with my mother's grim fate on my own." It was difficult to even look at him knowing that he may not be mine much longer. Hadn't I had enough devastation for one day?

∗   ∗   ∗

I had lied. I never anticipated facing my mother alone—so when I arrived to the Montana airport, I called the one person I had never pictured ever speaking to again, Travis.

It wasn't a surprise that he answered my call or that he quickly agreed to come pick me up even though we hadn't spoken a word in months.

He looked good, sun kissed and taller than ever.

"Travis," I whispered as he neared.

"Jac," he returned my whisper, embracing me slowly.

"I stopped by your place about a month ago," Travis admitted.

"You did?"

He nodded, smirking. "No one was home. I was looking for a Walking Dead marathon partner."

I smiled. "I should have told you I moved."

"I shouldn't have turned my back on you—we all make mistakes."

His confession took me by surprise.

"So, where are you living nowadays?" Travis asked as we weaved our way through the airport.

"Hawaii…" I answered softly, wondering if he would be able to put two and two together.

"Isn't that where Lee was from?" Ding-ding-ding.

"Is from—we live together." I looked up through lowered lashes, afraid of his reaction.

"Oh, wow." I had literally shocked him to silence.

"There's a lot we need to catch up on."

After leaving the airport I shared with Travis about my mother's condition and asked if he would accompany me to say goodbye. Travis agreed, not surprising me in the least.

"So what changed?" Travis asked as we parked the car.

"I found someone who wouldn't give up on me." Even though it was the truth, it didn't make it any easier to say to someone like Travis.

*   *   *

She looked worse for wear—her skin sunken in, her bones protruding and she was weak, unable to sit up. The sight was more than depressing.

"Mom, I'm here," I took her fragile hand in mine, rubbing it gently.

Slowly her gaze rose to meet mine. "You made it."

"Of course I made it."

"I'm sorry for everything I ever put you through," she said weakly.

"Shhh, let's focus on the positives—I'm here now."

"Where is he?" She looked right past Travis, searching for Lee.

"He is back in Hawaii…he had some obligations he had to take care of." It was a complete understatement, but I didn't really care. "He sends his regards."

"Promise me you won't make the same mistakes I did." My mother weakly glanced up at me.

Tears began trailing down my face thinking of my dysfunctional childhood. "I promise."

"You always were the prettiest Lily in the valley." My mother stated, then breathed in deeply.

Life was so unfair. Hadn't I been punished enough?

"We should let her get her rest," Travis whispered.

"I'm not going anywhere." And I meant it. I didn't move a muscle the next few days. I was still holding her hand when she finally passed in her sleep. Quick and painless.

The minute she passed, a portion of my heart felt empty. She was still my mother…no one should ever have to experience the pain associated with such a travesty.

After the tears had long since dried I finally left the hospital; Travis by my side.

"You never knew how much I loved you Jac, not once. And even though now is not the time, I can't let you leave this time without simply acknowledging it."

He wasted no more time before lowering his lips to mine firmly. He smelled of cologne; he smelled manly. Something was different about our kiss, I could feel the urgency radiating off his lips. He was leaving me breathless.

"You can't deny how well we go together," he stated after breaking off the kiss, leaving my mind hazy.

He was right…and for once it was hard to see that as a problem.

Thirty – Help, I'm Falling and I Can't Get Up

Lee

Jacqueline's absence was not easy on me. I missed her more than I ever knew possible. And with the way we left things, it left me feeling uneasy. I wanted to be there for her; to hold her hand through her mother's passing—but if I was a father, I wanted to be there for my son. I felt conflicted and torn.

The possibility of not knowing I had a son for half a decade left my stomach in knots. The paternity test results were supposed to be available on Monday. It was Saturday and to get my mind off Jacqueline, I focused it on the only other thought in my head—Tanner. I called up Ainsley and requested a meeting with the little guy—I had to know.

Ainsley suggested a play date at a nearby park and in no time I was pulling up to the park in my silver BMW. I could see her long brown hair whipping around her as she pushed Tanner on the swing. I squinted my eyes to attempt to get a better look at him from the safety of my car; my heart racing.

Even though I had requested the meeting, it didn't mean that I wasn't deathly afraid of it. Kids scared the shit out of me. Yeah, I could play like a kid—but raising them and knowing what they really needed? I was the epitome of clueless.

What would he think of me? Would he blame me for her choice? What if Tanner hated me? The thoughts inside my head were running wild.

Taking a deep breath, I reached for my door handle and exited my car. It was a gorgeous July afternoon in Kauai. The heat might have been unbearable, but the island had a great breeze snaking its way through. I waved as soon as Ainsley noticed me. She smiled back warmly.

"Tanner, there is somebody I'd like you to meet, Mr. Lee." I was crouching in front of the swing with my big hand outstretched.

"Hi," Tanner replied quickly before diving underneath my arm and to the seesaw.

"Oh, okay…" I chuckled uncomfortably.

"Well?" Ainsley nudged me with her elbow.

I glanced at her, my eyebrows raised.

"He obviously can't work that by himself. You want to take this one, or should I?" She motioned with her eyes and head towards Tanner who was impatiently waiting for one of us to join him.

"Oh, I definitely have this." I said before hopping on the seesaw for ten minutes and having a blast watching Tanner laugh from joy. Having children before I was fully ready had always been one of my biggest fears, but for one moment, a brief short-lived moment, I forgot why I had been so afraid in the first place. For one time in my life, I entertained the idea of being a father…and it didn't make me shit my pants.

I spent the next two hours playing with Tanner and Ainsley until the sun went down and I literally had to carry Tanner to the car because he had passed out from all the fun. I placed him in his car seat and let Ainsley buckle him in, closing the door lightly after she finished.

"Thank you for this, seriously," I said softly.

"No problem, really," She replied, staring at me a little too deeply in my eyes.

"Can I ask you a question?" I just had to know.

"Sure."

"Why did you do it?" It had been eating me alive since she told me the shocking news.

"Do what?"

"If you even had an idea that he was mine five years ago...why didn't you tell me? Why did you allow me to live my life with no knowledge of that possibility? Don't you think that's unfair Ainsley?" My voice had raised as I continued...I hadn't realized just how much her reckless decision had affected me.

"You weren't ready for a kid," she said simply.

"Maybe not, but that didn't give you the right to make that decision for me."

"You're right. I thought I knew what was best for him. And at the time I couldn't get you to commit to me—so I followed my instincts. But over the years I began to realize how unfair it was for me to punish Tanner for your hasty actions back in the day." She stepped closer to me, her voice lowering. "I made a mistake—forgive me?"

"What are you and Tanner up to tomorrow night?" I asked.

"What did you have in mind?"

"Miniature golf and pizza sound good?" It felt nice to be a kid again, even if it was short-lived.

"I'm sure Tanner will adore you even more after tomorrow."

"That is the plan..." I opened her car door for her, not wanting to lead her on. Luckily she caught on real quick.

"What time tomorrow?"

"Pick ya up at six?" I grinned at her through the open window.
"We'll be ready." And then the purr of the engine became audible and before I knew it she was gone.

*   *   *

The night of golfing and pizza had been exactly what I needed. As much fun as I had, it didn't compare to my feelings for Jacqueline. And even though I still intended to be there for the little guy in whatever way possible, I wanted Jacqueline by my side for every step of the way.

"What are you thinking about?" Ainsley asked softly as she closed the car door after our night of fun.

"Oh, nothing much," I lied.

"Want to know what I'm thinking about?" Ainsley stepped closer as she said it. "How unnaturally natural it is that we are here now. How right it all feels."

Uh-oh. It was time and I wasn't sure how Ainsley would react to the truth.

She took yet another step towards me and reached out her hand for mine. "Oh come on, you can't deny what has been happening here."

It was now or never. "Look Ainsley, I have a girlfriend, someone I care very deeply about, her name is Jacqueline, ring a bell? I would never jeopardize our relationship for the possibility of another chance with you. I'm sorry, but I would just never do that." I took a defensive step backwards.

"Why would you want her when you could have this—family?" Ainsley asked, exasperated.

"She's my best friend…and don't get me wrong—I'll still be there for Tanner *if* he is my son, but as for you and me Ainsley, we were over a long time ago. We had our chance, it didn't work out."

She looked like I had broken her heart for the second time—it wasn't any easier the second time around either.

"I guess I will see you Monday then?" Her voice was icy now.

"I'll call you when the results come in." I mirrored her tone unintentionally.

She quickly climbed into her car and sped off angrily.

I pulled my phone out of my pocket and eyed the time, it was a little after nine. Knowing that Montana was three hours ahead, I was sure my girlfriend would be asleep at this early hour. I dialed her familiar number anyways.

She answered on the fourth ring—right before I lost hope, her voice deep and tired. "Hello?"

"I'm sorry--did I wake you?" I asked.

"Mmm." Tell-tale sign she was not fully awake yet.

"Listen, just call me later when you wake up." As I went to hang up the phone her voice became easier to hear.

"No, you called me...what did you want?" Suddenly she sounded more alert.

"Come home, please. Everything here sucks without you. Our bed doesn't feel the same without you...I have no one to cuddle with at night. I'm begging you, please come home."

I paused waiting for a reply from her, but quickly decided to continue my groveling. "Gage has been missing you," I referred to my car. "And I might be missing you a little too."

"Just a little?" She finally spoke, pouting.

"Okay, maybe more like a lot."

"Come home," I begged again.

"Will you be waiting for me?" She asked, insecure.

"Of course. I'll always be waiting for you—I care about you." Okay, I more than cared, but I wanted to express that in person. It was intimate and I wanted it to remain so.

Thirty One – The L Word

Jacqueline

When I received the call from Lee asking me to return to Hawaii, the decision was one of the easiest ones I ever made. It was great to see Travis and to have his support through my mother's passing...but when it came to Travis and Lee—in my mind, there was no comparison.

Travis was there for me, most of my entire life, but when *I* needed him the most, he turned his back on me and walked away. Lee pushed me away most of the beginning of our relationship, but when I really needed him, he was there pushing *me* to be better. He knew I needed tough love—and he gave it to me while still being by my side.

Travis wasn't happy, which was to be expected, but we weren't on bad terms, and that's all I really cared about. He even saw me off to my flight, giving me the longest, tightest hug in the history of hugs. I took one long look at him before boarding my flight worried I may never see his handsome face again.

Lee was waiting for me when I finally made it in. He was beaming from ear to ear, I had never seen him so happy. "Welcome home baby," he whispered into my ear as he enveloped me in his arms.

"Are those for me?" I asked, not missing the fact that he had a bouquet of flowers hidden behind his back.

"Hey, no fair!" He pulled away quickly from me, shielding himself with the flowers. "I didn't even get to surprise you. You ruined it."

"They're beautiful," I smiled brightly, grabbing them from Lee and sniffing them. "Mmm, and they smell nice too."

"You're beautiful and smell nice," Lee added in a cheesy tone.

"And you're sucking up." I stuck out my tongue at him.

"I do have some groveling to do…believe me, it will come." He chuckled. "Did you check any bags?"

I shook my head. "We can go home."

I noticed his chest fall, his expression one of relief. "Did you think I wasn't going to come back?"

"I wasn't sure what to think. I was worried I had lost you for good. I'm sorry I was being stupid." Lee looked down at his shoes as he apologized.

"Hey," I said softly, tipping his chin towards me. "I missed you…a lot."

"I missed you too," he murmured before kissing me long and deep.

"Come on, let's go home."

"Say it again," he begged, his eyes fixated on mine.

"Let's go home…to our home." I repeated.

*　　*　　*

When I originally boarded that plane with Lee, I never expected my life to change so drastically. It had been less than three months since I had faced my fears and come out victorious with Lee at my side.

He was helping me experience a ton of new things—surfing, sky diving, zip-lining. Adventure was his calling. I wasn't as coordinated or brave—but I was willing.

We had been basically living together since day one like an old married couple, we even had sides of the bed and routines.

"You nervous about seeing Maddy soon?" I asked Lee, running my fingers through his buzzed hair. Madalynne and Parker's wedding was in less than two months and I wasn't even sure anymore how I felt about seeing Parker.

"Why would I be?" Lee asked, genuinely confused.

"Are you trying to say you don't have any feelings for her anymore?" I asked, grinning at him, attempting to call his bluff.

"No, that's not it." He pulled me in closer to him. "It's just that they don't hold a candle to my feelings for you."

I straightened myself up so I could look him in the eyes. "Mr. Bennett, are you trying to tell me something?"

His expression got stone cold serious then. "I love you," he whispered, barely audible.

"What was that? I can't hear you," I teased, sticking my tongue out at him.

He looked hurt. "You know how difficult this is for me…"

I inched closer to him, tracing his face lightly with my fingers. "Thank God Maddy made the terrible mistake of passing you up."

"Oh shut up!" He sighed, exasperated.

"No, I'm serious. I'm the luckiest girl in the world." I looked back at him, my eyes filled with love. We had been through so much separately and together it was a miracle we were even on speaking terms. From our pasts to the terrible way we treated one another in the beginning to growing together…it felt like we had known one another for a decade or longer. I could clearly state without a doubt that Lee was the person I cared most about in the world.

"You don't know how long I've been waiting to hear something like that…" Lee let out a long breath of air, I wondered how long he had been holding it in.

"Hey, look at me." I lifted his chin towards my face.

"I couldn't have dreamt something better up if I tried." Then I closed the distance between us.

Lee's lips were on mine faster than I could blink; one of his hands gently on the small of my back, and the other caressing my face as we kissed. The passion was growing with each part of our lips, each nibble.

"God, you have no idea how much I missed you," Lee gasped, moving my hair away from my neck and instantly heading for my spot.

It didn't take long, he had me hotter than hot. I pushed him onto the bed, which he toppled over onto.

"Bad girl," he said, grinning naughtily.

"Do I get a spanking?" I perched myself on the bed so I was on all fours, my ass in the air, pointed directly at Lee.

"You are so bad," Lee hissed, grinning. He grabbed me and threw me underneath him, my back was now flat on the bed. He kissed me again then roughly.

Whatever game we were playing was being enjoyed thoroughly by the both of us.

Lee ripped off my tank top and bra without another word. So, I followed suit removing his shirt.

He took it upon himself to cover whatever exposed parts of my body he came across with kisses and licks. It was just about driving me nuts.

He began kissing me passionately and deeply and then I felt one of his hands massaging me downstairs.

I was beyond wet, and soon enough Lee and I would be closer than ever. Our sex was always mind-blowing, passionate, and wild.

Without any more wasted time both our bottoms had been removed and Lee was in the process of removing my thong.

"Is this new?" He asked, holding it out by his index finger over the side of the bed.

I nodded, blushing.

"Did you buy it for me?"

I nodded again, remaining mute.

He threw it on the ground and then kissed me suddenly. His hand was between my legs, making sure I was ready for him to enter me.

I threw my head back, exhaling loudly. It all felt so good. He always felt so good.

Between my thighs was burning, in a good way as he thrusted in and out, in and out. He sped up his pace and I found myself moaning louder. It wouldn't be much longer.

I couldn't help myself, he already knew—but in the moment, it all became that much clearer. "I love you."

I must have said the magic words because seconds later Lee was convulsing in a positive way, moaning happily.

"I'll take that as you love me too?"

He was still panting, attempting to catch his breath—but he managed to pick up his head long enough to look me in the eyes. "You have no idea how long I have been wanting to tell you. How long you have been driving me crazy…"

"Crazy in a good way, I hope!"

He chuckled, letting his head drop again. "I love you, you crazy nut."

So we were dysfunctional—but there was passion—and it was off the charts.

I was going to love him forever...

Thirty Two – Blunt Honesty & Marriage Proposals

Lee

"Well…are you just going to sit there staring at it or are you going to open it?" Jacqueline broke the silence after nearly five minutes.

I always knew the day would come…I even thought at one point I was prepared for it; judgment day. But instead I found myself scared shitless. It was a catch-22. If I was Tanner's father, I had a son! But I had missed out on five years of his life. If I wasn't his father, Ainsley would have disrupted my relationship with Jacqueline for nothing. I couldn't help feeling a little resentful towards her.

I had been holding the unopened letter as if it were a piece of gold; delicate and lightly. The pit in my stomach growing deeper with each passing moment I wasted.

"Oh hell!" Jacqueline leaned forward and ripped it out of my hands quickly.

"Don't!" I yelped, lunging for it.

"Then grow a pair and open the damn thing," Jacqueline replied, handing the letter back to me.

"Fine," I sighed huffily. "But just remember you asked for it." And then I ripped the damn thing open once and for all. Shakily, I pulled out the contents inside hoping my fear wasn't as noticeable as it appeared to be. I swallowed deeply as I began to unfold the paper.

I felt my stomach dip a little. "He's not my son…" Conflicting emotions were swirling inside me.

Jacqueline's long release of breath was hard to miss. "You okay?"

I wasn't sure of the correct response. In fact, I wasn't sure whether I was supposed to be happy, sad, pissed, or remorseful. The only thing I was sure about was I needed Ainsley as far away from my relationship as possible.

"Excuse me for a second, I need to make a phone call." I kissed my girlfriend on the top of her head and stood up from the kitchen table, making my way out to the front porch.

I pulled out my cell phone, dialing Ainsley's number.

"Hello?" Her greeting was so unassuming.

"I got the results." No pleasantries…I couldn't help but feel slighted.

"You did…" she didn't sound surprised.

"He's not mine Ainsley. Tell me the truth…did you know?"

"What? No! How could you ever think such a thing?" Her voice rose apprehensively.

"Who's his father?" Call it curiosity—call it looking out for the kids well-being, but I wanted to know. I thought it was the least I deserved after the roller coaster she had put me through.

"Lee, I really thought he was yours…" She was avoiding the question expertly.

"Ainsley…"

"The other possibility isn't pretty," she replied, sounding choked up.

"What have you not told me?" I pushed, wanting answers.

"Do you even remember the last month of our relationship? How checked out I was? How easy I made it on you to dump me? Convenient don't you think? You want the truth? Here's the truth, I am only going to say it once—please don't make me repeat myself..." She inhaled deeply then said, "I was raped. Fourth of July, you were stuck working and I decided to attend a frat party by myself...bad choice it turned out."

"You're telling me this *now?*" All these years I never gave much thought to our breakup, justifying it because she made it so easy on me. I never stopped to think she might be hurting or in danger. I just moved on—what a grade A character I was...

"Lee, I never meant to come in between your relationship. I hope you believe me. Tanner deserved a father and I always hoped and prayed it was you. I didn't want to have to face the other reality." She was doing a hell of a job making me feel like an asshole.

"Look Ainsley, you didn't deserve a lot of the things I put you through, you're a good person and deserve so much better. I'm sorry I wasn't there for you back then and I'm sorry I'm not Tanner's father."

"Good luck with everything Lee, really. You deserve happiness too." Her voice sounded distant, sad.

"You've done a great job raising Tanner up until this point...you don't need anyone's help. You are his mom and his dad, never forget that." I wasn't sure when I became so wise, but I was rolling with the punches.

"Thanks."

"Goodbye Ainsley." I didn't wait for her to reply before hanging up the call and heading back into my house.

Jacqueline was sprawled out on the bed, nose in a book. She lowered the book slightly as she caught me approaching. "How did it go?"

"Can I be honest with you?"

She nodded. "Always."

"I don't even know what I am supposed to feel. I don't even know what a normal reaction is anymore."

"Let's just take it one day at a time," Jacqueline offered up.

I took the book out of her hands, throwing it to the ground with a thud.

"Marry me." I didn't know what came over me, but I was running with it. I had been there for Jacqueline so many times in the past and finally, we had reversed titles—she became my rock. She became my sanity.

"Excuse me?" She asked, choking lightly as I advanced upon her.

"Marry me," I repeated in almost an identical tone, now straddling her on the bed.

"We're basically married already—we live together," Jacqueline giggled nervously. After I remained silent for a few moments she piped up again. "When do you want to do this?"

"Get married? Can you not even say the words?" I poked her in the side and then hopped off her, sitting on the edge of the bed.

"I don't know…but I know I want to do it right," I responded.

"What do you mean?"

"It means I want to formally ask you." I pushed a few strands of her blond hair out of her face.

I wasn't sure how or when, but I had never felt so strongly about anything before…I wanted to spend the rest of my life with Jacqueline Blunt. Marriage used to scare the crap out of me…but after the paternity scare, nothing compared. I wasn't afraid of anything anymore. I trusted Jacqueline enough to give her my heart with hope that she would protect it.

She was still so young with so much life left to live. Tying her down almost seemed like a bad decision, but I loved her so God damn much I couldn't imagine my life without her in it. But as much as I needed her, she needed me—she needed someone stable in her life, someone who was aware of her condition and knew how to handle it. She needed me.

Thirty Three – The Beautiful Ending to a Dysfunctional Love Story

Jacqueline

The greenery, the hippies, the rain. Yep, we were definitely in Oregon. Lee and I decided to come a few days early to explore and have fun before the inevitable ceremony.

"Where are we again?" I asked curiously as I took in our surroundings.

"It's called Zena Church—Maddy told me about it once…"

"Oh great, I trusted you and you brought me to a haunted church and cemetery!" I smacked him across the shoulder.

"It's kind of hot, don't you think?" Lee asked, licking his lips.

"Oh no! You better slow your roll mister! I am not and will not get down and dirty here." I stood firmly, prepared to stand my ground.

Lee took one look at my surprised face and broke out into a round of chuckles. "Are you scared?"

What kind of question is that? Yes, yes I'm scared," I replied angered.

"You don't trust me to protect you?" Lee asked with a droopy lip.

"Of course I trust you ass," I retorted. "I just don't trust the world apart from you."

"Want to go back to the hotel?"

"Yes please," I answered quickly.

"Okay party pooper—have it your way," Lee joked, laughing at his own smart remark.

We climbed back into our rental car and Lee began back towards civilization.

"What are you looking to get into now?" I asked, sticking my tongue out playfully in his direction.

"I don't need a plan or structure babe, that's what's so great about me—I'm versatile, I go with the flow."

"My adventure man," I said squeezing his arm.

"Honestly, as long as I'm with you, I feel invincible—like I can do anything."

He had to know he had the same effect on me.

It wasn't a surprise that I was slightly nervous to see Parker—to meet Madalynne for the first time, but I was ready to take the next step towards my new relationship with Lee.

As soon as we hit the first set of steps I caught Lee letting out a big exhale of air.

"You sure you're ready for this?" I wasn't even sure I was.

Lee swallowed loudly. "We have each other— we can do this."

I smiled back at his fearlessness.

Madalynne and Parker had decided to forgo the festivities and simply make it official before he deployed. They still needed witnesses and thought it would be a good setup early on. They had no clue how right they had been.

For the longest time Parker was my every thought, my every dream. And when he came to Montana to visit me, I thought we would finally get our chance. But then he broke my heart—Travis left me shortly after—and I was left fragile. Lee was there to pick up the pieces. He pieced me back together. He knew how to calm me like no other.

Their figures came into focus before their faces did. They were both grinning ear to ear, they looked happy.

Lee squeezed my hand as we approached the pair, letting me know I wasn't alone—we were in this together.

"Aren't you guys the cutest thing ever?" Madalynne exclaimed as she wrapped her arms around us both.

"Hey man, sorry about your face," Parker laughed uncomfortably.

"It's water under the bridge," I heard Lee say. That deserved a squeeze.

As I hugged Parker for the first time in what felt like forever, I watched as Lee embraced Maddy. I wondered if he was feeling the same mix of emotions as I was.

"Can I talk to you for a minute?" Parker asked as he released me.

"Sure." I nodded as he led the way out of the chapel.

"I want to apologize for leading you on—for hurting you," Parker said softly.

"Parker, you've already apologized for that, remember?" I couldn't deny what an utterly good guy he was.

"I know, it just kills me to think I could have caused you any pain…you need to know that."

"I do know that—if it wasn't for your persistent fiancé I wouldn't have met Lee. I really have you guys to thank."

"Are you happy?" Parker—still trying to be the hero.

"Lee is amazing. And even though I really cared about you and was hurt, he is the perfect person for me."

"Madalynne the Matchmaker. Kind of has a ring to it, don't you think?" Parker laughed.

"I wouldn't go that far," I giggled. "You ready for this?"

Parker inhaled sharply then smiled. "As ready as I'll ever be."

*   *   *

His mischievous glances and grins were about to drive me nuts. I was returning the advances with a stink eye—if the officiant wasn't so hard of hearing and oblivious in general we may have been stripped our titles as witnesses.

"I now pronounce you husband and wife—you may kiss the bride," the officiant said; my stomach dipped with the realization that this was the end of a chapter. As bittersweet as dark chocolate.

Madalynne and Parker kissed in a quick, classy way, one that wouldn't rub it directly in our faces.

"Hold up," I heard Lee's voice as soon as the two parted.

"I've been wanting to tell you something for a really long time…I just wasn't sure of the right time or right words to convey what I was feeling." Lee addressed me in front of the others.

"I thought I knew what I wanted in life before you...I used to enjoy the variety of women, the endless privileges. A lot of those women were pushovers—you pushed me back, challenged me." Lee stepped closer to me then, taking both my hands in his.

"I always knew the extent to how much you needed me in your life—but I never fully digested the extent to how much I needed you. I needed you to remind me of the person I used to be...the person I can be again."

Just as I began to open my mouth to respond I noticed Lee was still going. His display of affection was not something I was used to, but I let myself enjoy it fully.

"Even though you irritate me, aggravate me, frustrate me, and annoy me to no end—there's no one else in the world I would rather spend my days with. I love you Jacqueline Marie Blunt."

My stomach dipped as I watched Lee drop to one knee. "Will you marry me?"

"Now?" I asked, my eyes darting around the room.

"What better time Jac?" He posed the obvious question.

"You're going to be stuck with me," I whispered so only he could hear.

"There ain't anyone else I'd rather be stuck with." He kissed my forehead then looked at me expectantly. "So—ready to be Mrs. Bennett?"

I took a few deep breaths before stepping forward, lacing my arm through his. "Let's do this."

Epilogue

Lee

I was nursing a broken heart when I met her—as was she. The mixture was like oil and water, we couldn't have been more different—but there was something to her spiciness, her unstableness—it was raw, and it was beautiful.

Jacqueline

He was my medicine. For so many years doctors had me on endless medication, "numbing" my problems—but what it really did was silenced me. I became a shell of myself.

And then I met Lee and he taught me how to live. He became my cure. Before him, I was convinced things like that didn't happen except in fairy tales. He proved me wrong at every turn. He gave me hope in the darkness.

Preview of the fourth and final book in the Infinite Love series, *Against All Odds*:

One – From the First Moment I Laid Eyes on You

Austyn

We lock eyes from across the room and I quickly blush, breaking the stare. His green eyes have me entranced for a moment too long there.

I feel an arm snaking around my neck and my nose scrunches up in fake disgust. "Better quit that, or people will think we are together!" I playfully push my cousin Lee away from me.

"What? You don't find this attractive?" He looks offended, but only slightly.

I can't help but smile. "You're disgusting, you know that?" I turn my attention back on the mysterious cutie across the room, hoping he didn't catch Lee's dumb move from a few seconds ago.

I can't be too upset with Lee, he's the reason we are on this adventure to begin with. He's always been the big brother I never had; providing for me whenever necessary. He was able to get me out of college for a week, so I am forever grateful.

I've never been to the Bahamas before. I've never really been out of the state of California, so the trip has me all sorts of anxious. I can't wait to break out our stash of alcohol we so swiftly snuck into our cabin, but all in good time. Lee and I are on the observation deck as the ship pushes off.

"Don't look now, but I think someone has the hots for you," Lee whispers into my ear.

I can't help looking around wildly, hoping it is the cutie from earlier. "Where?"

"Don't make it obvious or anything." Lee chuckles to himself.

I elbow him in the chest when he least expects it, causing him to back up in surrender. "I'm just being a good wing man."

"Seriously." Again my eyes scan the room madly. "Which one was it?"

That dumb ass is smiling back, knowing he has the upper hand as always.

"You're an ass—you know that right?" He always finds a way to piss me off. I begin to walk away when I feel him grab my arm to stop me.

"He's going to be too intimidated with me standing here with you. I'm going to go to the room, and why don't you invite him back—we can drink and get to know him in a laid back atmosphere."

"Which one?" I ask for what I hope to be the last time.

"Skater boy," he spits out before turning around and heading to our cabin.

I sneak a glance across the deck one more time. The stranger's eyes are fixated on me. My heart begins racing as I slowly make my way across the observation deck towards the hippie looking male. To my surprise, he sees me approaching and begins to make his way towards me; we end up meeting in the middle.

He has longer shaggy blond hair and the most piercing green eyes. I find myself searching for my words.

"Hey, how's it going?" he finally breaks the uncomfortable silence, smiling, his eyes twinkling as he does so.

"Hi." I smile politely. "I'm Austyn."

"Avery," he replies, his eyes intently on mine. "So—the Bahamas..." he fills in the awkward silence. "Ever been before?"

I shake my head as if to say no. "You?"

"This is my third time," he answers like it is such a normal thing.

I'm only nineteen and therefore still young, but this angers me somehow.

"Listen, you want to grab a drink?" Avery asks, unaware I am not of legal age.

"Actually yeah." I nod. "I snuck some aboard with me—want to come back to my room?" I am positive he saw Lee earlier. He would have had to have been blind to miss him.

"Even better." He claps his hands together and we begin walking back in unison.

*   *   *

It's a strange feeling being watched, yet one I have become accustomed to. One I lust for. His green eyes can pierce through me like no one else's. My senses are heightened; he is winning the game as always.

I'm supposed to be upset with him; angry with him. I'm supposed to be giving him the cold shoulder but Avery Phillips knows exactly how to make me forget why I am even mad at him in the first place with little to no effort. To say he has complete control over me is an understatement. I'm not even sure how I made it through my life prior to him entering it. He changed everything with one charming smile.

"I know you're awake," I hear him whisper through my tightly squeezed eyes.

My lips curl up into an uncontrollable smile, my eyes slowly opening. "I'm supposed to be mad at you."

Then it comes…that damn charming smile— the one that breaks me every time. "Do you even remember why you were angry with me in the first place?"

Of course I do, but when I open my mouth to speak all I can manage to do is stumble over my words.

"That's what I thought." He chuckles.

Even though Avery chooses to grow his hair out and sometimes experiments with his facial hair, he is still a very handsome guy, rugged and wild.

I feel his warm breath on the back of my neck, the crook of my shoulder, sending chills down my spine. His arms wrap around my waist from behind, pulling me into him. I feel him bury his face into my short hair, inhaling me.

"You know I hate going to bed mad," he says softly.

I turn so we are now face to face, running my fingers down the side of his cheek lightly. "I'm sorry. I promise I won't do it again."

He smirks. "Good." And then he lowers his lips to mine slowly and eagerly.

We've been dating for over six years, and while I am ready for commitment, it appears Avery has more important things on his mind. It's not that he doesn't love me…I don't doubt that for a second—it's just that he isn't quite ready to grow up yet.

Avery was the first person to make me feel important; to make me feel safe. I want the happily ever after with him—the white picket fence, the house, the children, and the pets. I want it all. Although, for as far back as I can remember that was all I wanted in my very core.

Before Avery, I didn't know my worth. I let guys walk all over me because it's what I thought I deserved. A normal relationship to me was riddled with unhealthy jealousy and cheating. By the time Avery found me, I was a shell of myself. I knew the girl I used to be and I fought against the current to get back there; Avery helped me succeed. He saw the beauty in my core even when I didn't anymore.

"Hey, where did you go just now?" Avery asks softly, stroking my hair.

I kiss him then, fast and strong, taking him by surprise. He melts into me as he pulls me in deeper, closer. The passion is something I look forward to.

His hands find the elastic waistband of my sweatpants within seconds, one of them makes its way under and beneath my sheer undies.

Let's just say he has mad skills.

*   *   *

It's the first day Avery and I have had off together in a long time so we decide to make the most of it. We head out early for the Saturday market. We haven't had the chance to go often, but it's one of our favorite things to do together. We love getting fresh fruit and vegetables, bartering, and checking out all of the vendors.

We meet our mutual friends, Tyler and Liv there. They're a married couple we've been spending time with since we began dating. We were even in their wedding party. Tyler and Avery met first when Avery used to play out at open mic nights. They hit it off and the rest is history. Liv is one of the only girls I've really gotten along with. Most girls are too catty for my taste, but we complement each other.

Liv slides her arm through mine and pulls me ahead of the guys. "I have to tell you something…" she whispers as we walk through the market.

I lower my ear to her mouth and whisper back, "What?"

She glances back at the guys to make sure they are lost in their own conversation, which they are…something about Apple loading U2's entire album onto all their devices and how much of a travesty it is…

"I'm pregnant!"

My eyes widen at her confession. "Oh my God!" I squeal. The guys don't even notice. "Does Tyler know yet?"

She shakes her head wildly. "No, and I want you to help me think of a cute way to tell him."

I'm so excited for my friend that I am grinning like an idiot from ear to ear, but I can't help feeling a tinge of jealousy. Tyler and Liv seem to have the most perfect relationship. They're married and now starting a family…something I've always wanted. Avery loves me…I don't doubt that for a second, but anytime I bring up marriage or a family, he shuts down. I get that he isn't ready…but we've been together for over five years—half a decade. If he isn't ready now, is he ever going to be?

The guys are trailing behind us still engaged in an entertaining conversation when an idea pops into my head. "Get a bag of buns and then put one into the oven. When he gets home tell him there is something sweet in the oven. Get it? A bun in the oven!"

Liv breaks out into a wide grin. "I knew I could count on you!"

A gust of wind blows past us, ruffling her curly blond hair. "Now you guys need to catch up."

I shoot a quick glance back at Avery. "Yeah…Avery seems to be on his own time schedule. I don't know if that will happen."

Liv takes notice of the sad tone in my voice. "You guys are perfect together, Austyn. And he loves you. Honestly, as long as you're happy, there's no reason to rush anything. You have your entire life ahead of you."

I smile back at her. "I just wish he wanted to marry me…"

She wraps her arm around my shoulder, giving it a reassuring squeeze. "Oh, he does. He just doesn't know it yet."

I chuckle as I see the guys come up on our sides.

"What are you guys talking about?" Tyler asks, throwing his arm around Liv's waist and pulling her into him.

"Oh, nothing," she replies, and we both share a secret smile.

God, I hope she's right about Avery…

About the author:

Krista Pakseresht has always been a dreamer. From the first time she opened her eyes. Creating worlds through words is one thing she is truly talented at. She specializes in Young adult/New adult romance, horror, action, fantasy, and non-fiction under the pen name Kira Adams. She is the author of the Infinite Love series, the Foundation series, the Darkness Falls series, and the Looking Glass series.